NEW YORK TIMES BESTSELLING AUTHOR TRACEY JANE JACKSON WRITING AS

PIPER DAVENPORT

Primal Howl

BOOK 1 IN THE PRIMAL HOWLERS MC SERIES

2019 Trixie Publishing, Inc.
Copyright © 2019 by Piper Davenport
All rights reserved.
Published in the United States

Sale of this book without a front cover may be unauthorized. If this book is coverless, it may have been reported to the publisher as "unsold or destroyed" and neither the author nor the publisher may have received payment for it.

Primal Howl is a work of fiction. Names, characters, places, and incidents are the products of the author's imagination and are used fictitiously. Any resemblance to actual events, locales, or persons, living or dead, is entirely coincidental.

Cover Art
Jack Davenport
Trixie Publishing, Inc.

TRIXIE
PUBLISHING

ISBN-13: 9781087812045

Liz Kelly:
Thanks again. Your insight is always so spot on!

Jack:
Thanks for being my muse, and really great in bed!

Gail
You are a scholar and a saint, and I ADORE you!

Brandy
Thanks for keeping the timelines and characters straight. You are godsend!

All it took was one page and I was immediately hooked on Piper Davenport's writing. Her books contain 100% Alpha and the perfect amount of angst to keep me reading until the wee hours of the morning. I absolutely love each and every one of her fabulous stories. ~ **Anna Brooks – Contemporary Romance Author**

Get ready to fall head over heels! I fell in love with every single page and spent the last few wishing the book would never end! ~ **Harper Sloan, NY Times & USA Today Bestselling Author**

Piper Davenport just reached deep into my heart and gave me every warm and fuzzy possible. ~ **Geri Glenn, Author of the Kings of Korruption MC Series**

This is one series I will most definitely be reading!! Great job Ms. Davenport!! I am in love!! ~ **Tabitha, Amazeballs Book Addicts**

For the REAL Razzle!

Raquel, thank you for being such an amazing flight attendant and sharing your story! You are gorgeous!

Raquel

About two months ago...

"ARE YOU READY?" Sierra, my best friend and roommate, bellowed up the stairs of the town-house we shared.

"Give me a sec!" I called back as I unplugged my curling iron, hearing her footsteps as she rushed upstairs.

She peeked her head into my bathroom. "Come on, slowpoke. I want to get my drink on."

I chuckled. "Keep your panties on, I'm coming."

"I'm not wearing panties."

"Gross, Sierra, I did *not* need to know that."

My bestie wore a black leather mini skirt, knee-high boots, and a tight pink, deep V-neck t-shirt that hugged every curve. I was dressed a little more conservatively in a pair of dark skinny jeans, knee-high boots, and a Harley-Davidson t-shirt that hid my squishy bits nicely.

We were heading to Smiley's in Colorado Springs, a notorious biker bar on the edge of town. My brother happened to be the president of the Dogs of Fire MC in Savannah, so I was pretty familiar with the establishment and who frequented it. The building welcomed everyone, and it was considered sacred, neutral ground, so the bikers tended to behave themselves.

"I'm hoping to find me a sexy biker to fuck me against the wall," Sierra said.

"*Sierra!*" I admonished. "You promised you'd be good."

She grinned. "Oh, I plan to be."

I rolled my eyes. "Good lord, woman, behave."

"No. What does your brother say?"

"Well behaved women don't get shit done," I said, sliding lipgloss onto my lips.

She sighed. "I wish Tristan was single."

I smiled. "A lot of people do."

Tristan was my older, half-brother. His father had married my mother a few years after his first wife, Tristan's mom, died. I was just as close, if not closer, to him than my full-blooded younger brothers, and he was often my rock when I needed someone to lean on.

I smiled. "A lot of people do."

"Are you sure he's committed to Olivia?"

I laughed. "Honey, not even Liv can run from Tristan, and believe me, she's tried. He is totally devoted to her."

Sierra sighed. "I want a man like that."

"You'll find one," I said.

"Brando's legal now, right?" she asked.

"If you mean, legal to drink, yes. He's twenty-one."

"Corwin's prettier though."

"Down tiger, he's only nineteen."

"Damn," she hissed, and I smiled.

Both my baby brothers were already heartbreakers, but she was right. Corwin had model good looks, where Brando was more rugged. But, really, the difference was whether you liked Ashton Kutcher more than Channing Tatum. Corwin was lean and tall, whereas Brando was still tall but built like a brick shithouse.

"Does Tristan know you're going to Smiley's without 'protection'?" she asked.

"He won't care."

"That's a no," she retorted.

"I'm twenty-four years old, I don't need to tell my brother anything."

"Um, okay, sure, we can play it that way," she said. "If he finds out, though, I'm playing dumb."

"It's fine. I know Smiley. He'll watch out for us." I faced her again. "I'm ready."

"Good. I already called for a car."

We headed outside and the ride share was already waiting for us. The bar wasn't far, but the driver still wasn't sure about leaving us. "This is rough place," he said in broken English.

"We've been here before," I said, pushing open my door. "Thanks, though."

Sierra followed me out and we walked inside, met at the door by a giant of a man.

"IDs." We handed our IDs to him, then he glanced at us, handing them back. "You sure you're in the right place?"

I smiled. "We're good."

"You run into issues, you let me know."

"Okay, thanks."

Moving through the crowd, we sidled up to the bar and Smiley walked over to us. "Hey, beautiful."

"Hey, Smiley," I said.

"Does Doc know you're here?" he asked.

"What's with everyone thinking I need to tell Doc everything?"

He smirked. "Well, you be careful."

"We will," I promised.

"What can I get you?"

"Shots," I said. "Patrón, please."

"Put it on my tab," a guy from our left said. He was creepy looking, his slicked back hair giving him a greasy look, and I planned to stay as far away as possible.

"No, that's okay," I said.

"I insist."

I sighed. "I appreciate it, but it's really okay."

"Bitch—"

"Don't call her a bitch, asshole," Sierra hissed.

"There a problem here?" a tall, sexy as fuck biker asked. He had his arms crossed, so I couldn't see the patch on his cut, but it could say Satan's Devils and I wouldn't care. Lordy, he was pretty. Blond hair, a little longer on top, fell onto his forehead and drew focus to his eyes, which were almost an ice blue. He had a full beard and I ached to run my fingers through it.

"What's it got to do with you?" Greasy demanded.

"Oh, I don't know, Stimpy, maybe because you're harassing my woman and she just got here."

"Oh, shit, Orion. Sorry, man. Didn't realize she was with you." Stimpy raised his hands and walked away.

Orion focused on me. "You good?"

"Yes. But you didn't need to do that."

Sierra leaned in close and without looking at her, I knew she was swooning.

4

"I know your brother, Raquel, I *did* need to do that," he said.

I forced myself not to react. "My brother?"

He smiled and I nearly lost my mind...and my panties.

"Doc," he said. "You know, the president of the Dogs of Fire Savannah."

"How could you possibly know Doc's my brother?" I asked. "I've never met you."

He leaned against the bar, now fully facing me and I craned my head to look up at him.

"My old man's the president of the Primal Howlers. I've known your brother for a while."

Of course he had.

"Yum," Sierra breathed out, for my ears only.

Orion pulled out his phone and swiped his finger over the screen. "I've got a picture of you from your Christmas party last year. I never forget a face." Handing me the phone, I saw the photo from the charity event the club put on every year, handing out presents to the foster kids in the area. I was standing beside my brother and laughing. I think he'd made some inappropriate joke right before the picture was snapped. "Plus, you look a lot alike."

I frowned. "Translation: Doc sent you this to keep an eye on me."

He slid his phone back in his pocket. "I plead the fifth."

"I've been here several times and I know Smiley well, so how come I've never seen you?"

"Because I didn't want you to see me."

I narrowed my eyes. "Have you been stalking me?"

"You can stalk me," Sierra said. "Anytime."

Orion grinned at her. "I'll keep that in mind."

"Patrón," Smiley said, setting shot glasses in front of us and pouring tequila into them.

Orion gave him a chin lift and Smiley nodded, refusing

to take my credit card.

"I've got this," Orion said.

"Um, no, you don't," I countered.

Smiley chuckled. "Like your spunk, sweetheart, but your money's no good here."

"So, we can drink as much as we want?" Sierra asked. "For free?"

"Go for it."

"Challenge accepted," she retorted, and Orion smirked.

I shook my head. "Sier—"

"Before we drink too much to care," Sierra said, "will you introduce me to your club members? Just in case I want to go home with someone…"

I groaned. "Sierra, seriously, put it back in your pants."

"You wanna come sit with us, you can," Orion offered, nodding to the tables where several of the Primal Howlers were congregating.

"Hell, yeah," Sierra answered immediately. "Show me the way to the testosterone."

She headed toward the group and Orion turned to follow, but I grabbed his arm and he faced me again. "She's impossible when she's drunk, so I don't want any of your guys taking advantage."

"They won't." Orion smiled. "But what about you?"

"What about me?"

"Are you impossible when you're drunk?"

I shrugged. "You'll have to get to know me better to find that out."

"I like a challenge."

"You think that now, but give it time," I retorted. "You'll change your mind."

He laughed as he led me to his group.

"Holy shit, Raquel?"

A tall man rose to his feet and grinned. He looked like Orion, only his hair was darker.

"I feel like I'm at a disadvantage," I grumbled. "Do y'all know who I am?" Everyone at the table nodded and I groaned. "Just when did Doc put the edict out to watch me?"

"Two years ago."

"Really?" I ground out. Right before I moved to Colorado. Of course he did.

"I'm Sundance," the man said, shaking my hand.

Orion chuckled and nodded to the man who was towering above me. "Sundance is the president."

That made sense. Orion looked just like his dad.

Indicating the man sitting in the chair next to Sundance, Orion said, "That's Rocky, our VP, next to him is Moses, our Sergeant, and the two practically fuckin' in that chair are Mozart and Nellie."

Nellie pushed off Mozart's lap and reached her hand out. "We don't get out much."

I smiled, shaking her hand. "It's nice to meet you."

"You too, sweetie."

"Has anyone ever climbed you?" Sierra asked Sundance. "I got an A in my mountaineering class, in case you were wondering."

Sundance dropped his head back and laughed. "You wanna climb me, baby, you feel free."

"See what I mean?" I glanced up at Orion. "That's after one shot."

Orion grinned. "It's all good. She's safe here."

I nodded. "I appreciate that."

* * *

Orion

Doc's baby sister was a fuckin' knockout in person. This could be a problem. Jesus Christ, her petite, curvy body could bring me to my knees and I'd happily genuflect for as long as she wanted me to.

When she and her friend walked in, I recognized her immediately, and knew she might be in trouble when Stimpy approached her. What came out of my mouth after that, was done while I was obviously in some kind of fugue state, because I'd never declared anyone as belonging to me, and certainly not in a place as public as Smileys.

Goddammit, that was not my smartest moment.

Because now she was marked as mine.

And I liked it.

* * *

Raquel

By the third shot of Patrón, I was feeling pretty loose. I blamed Orion and the way he made me feel. Safe. Relaxed. Accepted. I also blamed Sierra. She kept handing me shot glasses with the liquid deliciousness that I'd never been able to resist.

When she tried to hand me the fourth, I shook my head. "If I have another one, I'm gonna go home with someone."

"I'm good with that," Orion said. "If it's me."

I rolled my eyes. "Keep dreaming, big man."

He chuckled as he stood, then leaned down, whispering in my ear, "Baby, I'm your dream come true and you'll figure that out sooner than later."

I couldn't stop a shiver as I shook my head and laughed. God, I was hungry. I hadn't had sex in two years, and I was just tipsy enough to want Orion to whet that appetite. Or oil the creaks. Or get me wet *and* oily.

Oh, who was I kidding? I'd let that man oil me up even if I was sober.

I watched him walk up to the bar, his ass looking unbelievable in his Levis, and I imagined him taking me from behind. He returned with a beer, a grin from ear-to-ear, and leaned down again to whisper in my ear. "You keep lookin' at me like that, I'm gonna take you somewhere private."

I licked my lips. "Don't make promises you can't keep."

His eyes widened slightly, studying me for a few seconds before sitting down again.

"Why are you called Orion?" I asked.

He smiled. "Mom. She figured since our last name was Graves, she wanted me to remember to look at the stars, so she'd always call me Orion, instead of Adam."

"Adam Graves," I said. "That's a good, strong name."

He chuckled. "Yeah, I guess so. No one ever calls me by it, but I guess it's a good one."

"I like it." I smiled. "Do you have siblings?"

"Drake and Violet. Both younger, both a pain in the ass most of the time." He cocked his head. "Done with the twenty questions?"

"I haven't decided yet."

He grinned. "Give me your phone."

He turned his head toward me. "Give me your phone."

I raised an eyebrow. "Why?"

"Just give it to me." I handed him my phone and he typed something into it, then handed it back. "You've got my info now. Use it."

"For what?"

"Anything you want."

I pivoted to face him. "Anything?"

"Yeah, baby, anything."

I bit my lip and smiled. "You might regret saying that."

"Pretty sure I won't," he said, taking a swig of his beer.

"I'm gonna need you to stock up on condoms."

He spit his beer out and I laughed.

"Jesus Christ," he hissed as his biker buds turned to look at him.

"You okay?" Sundance asked him.

"Yeah, I'm good, Pops," he said, staring at me.

I grinned and took a sip of water, watching his eyes blaze with desire.

Yes, this man was going to WD-40 the shit out of my body.

Raquel

Two days later…

I ARRIVED HOME from class to find Orion leaning up against his bike, checking his phone, and I couldn't help my stomach from fluttering as I parked my car.

I climbed out and walked toward him. "Are you stalking me again?"

"Depends." He grinned, slipping his phone into his pocket. "Do you like surprise visits or should I expect a cop to arrive and escort me off the premises?"

"How did you know where I live?"

"Sierra slipped me your address before you left the bar the other night. She said something about you needin' your world rocked."

I rolled my eyes. "That woman needs to be leashed."

"I know a few guys who could do that for you."

I couldn't stop a laugh. "I may get their numbers from you later. What are you doing here?"

"It's a nice day. Was gonna see if you wanted to go for a ride."

"It's been ages since I've been on a bike," I breathed out.

"It's long overdue then."

"Let me grab a jacket."

"Sounds good."

I rushed inside the townhouse, dropped my bag on the floor, and rummaged through my closet for my old leather jacket. It was buried in the back, so I had to wrestle it out from under other coats on the floor.

Sierra was at work, so I sent her a quick text, then headed back to Orion and his gorgeous Harley-Davidson Fatboy. After shoving my purse into one of his saddle-bags, he handed me a helmet, and threw his leg over the seat. I climbed on behind him and we took off for the open road.

I wrapped my arms around his waist and took a deep breath, the thrill of being on the back of a bike surging through me as Orion expertly drove the back streets, then opened it up when we hit the freeway.

Lordy, I'd missed this.

We drove for a good twenty minutes before he pulled off and I knew exactly where we were headed.

"Oh my god, are we going to Billy's?" I yelled over the pipes.

"You good with that?" he called back.

12

"Hell, yeah!"

Billy's Old Style BBQ was the best place in town. It was a little out of the way and somewhat secluded, but anyone who knew anything about good food, knew about Billy's. I gave Orion a squeeze and he rubbed my arm quickly before continuing down the road. We pulled up to the old building ten minutes later, and I virtually jumped off the bike, suddenly starving.

Orion chuckled as he helped me with my helmet. "Eager, huh?"

"The second you said Billy's, my stomach was ready," I admitted. "I miss good BBQ."

"Well, that's high praise," he said. "I've lived here my whole life, so I've never known anything different."

"Trust me. Billy's a genius."

He grinned, pulling my purse from the saddlebag and handing it to me before taking my hand and leading me through the front doors of the restaurant.

The tall, blonde, thin, and model-esque hostess approached with a huge grin. "Hey, Orion."

"Hey, Whit," he said.

"Table for two?" she asked, raking her pornographic eyes over his body, never once looking at me.

"Yeah, that'd be good," he said.

"Friend of yours?" I asked, removing my hand from his as we navigated the narrow spaces between tables.

He didn't answer, shocker, as Whit sat us at a booth in the corner.

Handing us menus, she smiled at Orion, leaning down, obviously so he could get a glimpse of her teeny tiny cleavage. "Your server will be here shortly, but if you need anything, honey, let me know."

I mouthed, "Honey?" for his eyes only and Orion raised an eyebrow.

"Thanks, Whit," he said, and the slut walked away.

Why did guys always go for the rail thin blondes? And why the hell did I care? That was the bigger question, really. I was short and curvy, but I was in shape. I mean, round was a shape, technically.

"You okay?" he asked.

"Golden," I said, perusing my menu, even though I knew exactly what I wanted.

"You're not jealous, are you?"

I glanced at him. "Of whom?"

He chuckled, shaking his head. "No one."

I lowered my menu with a sigh. "Sorry. I'm not jealous in the sense that she was coming onto you so hard, I'm sure she'd drop to her knees and suck you off in the middle of this restaurant if you asked her to. It's more of a… I don't know… her being tall and blonde with a thigh gap to die for, the opposite of me, and sometimes girls just want what they can't have."

"You want to be tall and blonde?"

"And skinny," I said.

He smiled. "Well, that's dumb."

"Is it?"

"Yeah. You're a hundred times prettier than Whitney. She needs to eat a fuckin' sandwich, or twelve."

Oh my god, my stomach just dropped into my vagina. "Well, I don't know if that's necessarily true, but it's sweet of you to say."

"You don't believe a word I'm sayin', do you?"

I smiled. "I don't know you. So, no."

He laughed. "Okay, Razzle, I'm gonna change that."

"Razzle?"

"You get a little razzled when you're trying not to show me your emotions."

I wrinkled my nose. "I do not."

He hummed, focusing back on his menu. "Okay, Razzle, you don't."

"Did you stock up?" I asked, pretending to look at my food options. His quiet hiss indicated he knew exactly what I was asking, and I grinned as I met his eyes. "Well? Did you?"

"You serious about that?"

"As a heart attack," I said. "No strings, though. I'm not looking for a commitment."

"Jesus Christ," he hissed.

"You got a problem with that?"

"No."

"Good." I closed my menu and leaned across the table. "How's that for razzled?"

He dropped his head back and laughed.

* * *

The next day, Sierra was working, so I had the house to myself...which was why Orion was on his way over for our first night together. I wasn't nervous, surprisingly, but I *was* excited. Lordy, I needed some relief.

My doorbell rang and I rushed to the front door, smoothing my hair before pulling open the door. Before I could greet him, Orion had me pushed up against the wall and his mouth was on mine. I gripped his leather jacket and held on for dear life as his tongue explored mine and his hand slid to my waist.

He broke the kiss, settling his forehead to mine and smiling. "Hey."

"Hi," I breathed out, kissing him again, this time quickly. "You're early."

"Personality flaw."

I tugged his beard gently. "Not a flaw."

He chuckled. "You look gorgeous."

I wore a striped maxi skirt with a V-neck T-shirt tied at my waist. I'd taken care with my hair, blow drying the natural curl straight and had applied very little makeup.

"Thanks, so do you." I smiled up at him. "Are you hungry?"

"Not for food. You?"

I licked my lips. "Same."

"Yeah?"

I nodded. "Can we fuck now and eat later?"

He chuckled. "I plan to eat, baby, but it'll be you."

"Okay," I rasped. "Come on."

I led him up to my room and closed us in, just in case Sierra came home early. And then Orion's mouth was on mine and his tongue slid between my lips, and I wrapped my arms around his neck in an effort to stay upright. Before I could fully register what was happening, my shirt was gone, as was my skirt, leaving me in my bra and panties. My nipples started tingling as he unsnapped my bra from behind, tugging it from my body and dropping it on the floor.

His shirt was next, and I barely got a chance to take in his lean muscles and the Primal Howlers tattoo spanning his chest before I was on my back on my mattress and his face was buried between my legs.

My legs jolted as I slid them over his back and arched into his mouth, unable to stop a moan as his tongue found my clit over my panties.

Perfection.

He guided my legs back onto the mattress and slid my panties down, before throwing them in the corner and removing his boots and jeans. I watched him strip, biting my lip in an effort not to cry out in ecstasy at the vision of him naked. Lordy, he was pretty.

Tattoos covered his chest and neck, while his arms were bare. I found this both fascinating, and sexy as hell.

He smiled, running his hands up the outside of my thighs. "You are beautiful."

"You too," I rasped, and he pushed my legs apart, focusing on my pussy again.

He ran his tongue between my lips before moving to my clit and sucking gently, then blowing air onto the sensitive nub. I moaned as my body shivered deliciously at his touch.

I lost his mouth when he took a second to roll on a condom and I couldn't stop myself from sitting up and running my tongue over one of his tattoos right between his pecs, just above the Primal Howlers logo. He smiled, leaning down to kiss me again, then I was on my back and he was sliding into me.

"Jesus," he hissed. "You're fuckin' gorgeous."

I wrapped my legs around his waist, arching into him, taking him deeper, and he started to move. Slowly at first, but then faster, building a fire inside of me as he covered my mouth with his.

My arms and legs clenched around him as my body thrummed with an impending climax and I let out a quiet sigh.

"Wait for me," he demanded.

"Oh, god," I panted out. "I don't think I can."

He slammed into me, then twisted my nipple between his finger and thumb, and I cried out as I came apart around him. He groaned, then I felt his dick pulse inside of me. He rolled us to our sides, and I slid my leg over his hip to stay connected. "Wow."

Orion chuckled. "That was a little quicker than I would have liked."

"We've got all night," I reminded him.

"This is true." He stroked my cheek, running his thumb over my lips. "You're amazing, Razzle."

I kissed his thumb. "Back atya."

"You good with this being exclusive?"

I frowned. "I told you I didn't want a commitment."

"I get it, but I wanna get to a point where we don't

17

have to use condoms, and we can't do that if we're not exclusive."

"Oh, right. Good point."

"You on the pill?"

I shook my head. "IUD."

"I went to the clinic yesterday and took every test I could. Should have the results in a few days."

"I got tested when I ended it with Mark. I haven't been with anyone since, but I can go do that if you want."

"How long ago was that?"

"Right before I moved here."

"You haven't been with anyone for over two years?"

"Yes. Why, is that weird?" I asked.

"Yes."

"Why?"

"Because you're fuckin' sexy, Raquel."

I blushed. "Well, that's ridiculously sweet."

"It's the truth," he said. "You can't tell me men aren't falling at your feet."

"I *can* tell you that," I countered.

"Then they're idiots."

I snorted. "Stop."

"I bet you twenty bucks you're just not noticin'."

"Whatever. Can we get off this subject, please?"

"The subject of you being sexy as fuck?"

I nodded. "Yes. That one."

"We can once you acknowledge it."

"Oh my god, you're ridiculous."

He grinned. "Maybe so, but I'm not wrong."

"Okay, let's put aside the fact you're being super sweet right now, it's not just that guys aren't throwing themselves at me. I've been swamped with research. This is the first 'distraction' I've had in two years."

He raised an eyebrow. "Really?"

"Yep."

"I'm honored, Razzle."

I chuckled. "You should be."

"I want to know about your research, but hold that thought," he said, sliding out of me and heading to the bathroom. He returned, climbing under the covers and pulling me over his chest. "What are you researching?"

"The effects of pharmacology on behavior," I said. "Specifically, the effects of CBD on childhood seizures and nonverbal autism."

"What about adults with the same?"

"I'm focusing on children, but I'm sure whatever I find will work for adults as well."

"Which explains the move to Colorado."

I smiled, tracing his Howlers tattoo with my finger. "Exactly. I had the option to move to Washington, but Colorado seemed more my style."

"Let me guess. No Dogs here, ergo, more your style."

I chuckled. "You're smarter than you look."

"Been told that before."

I set my chin on my hand and met his eyes. "What about you?"

"What about me?"

"What's your story?"

"That's gonna have to keep for another day," he said, rolling me onto my back and kissing my neck. "I've got plans for you."

Did he ever.

By the time I fell asleep wrapped up in him, I was sure my body would never recover.

* * *

Orion

Raquel finally fell asleep about two a.m. I, on the other hand, couldn't do the same. Mostly because everything we'd done rocked me to my core. Jesus, she was incredible, and I had a feeling I was in trouble.

Now, her lush body was pressed against mine and she was quietly snoring. All I wanted to do was wrap myself around her and stay here forever. But I wouldn't. I had to keep this casual. Had to keep her at an arm's length. After talking to her for ten minutes, I realized she was far too good for my degenerate ass, and I refused to let my shit rub off on her.

The problem was, I'd buried myself deep and I'd never felt anything so perfect.

Scrubbing one hand down my face, the other wrapped firmly around Raquel, I contemplated my current predicament. I was supposed to make a run to Denver in the morning to check on a couple of our businesses. My club owned several cannabis shops in the area, not to mention, my father and I owned six of our own. I had been tasked with checking on the three we'd just opened in Denver, which meant I'd be out of pocket for at least a week.

And I didn't want to be out of pocket from Raquel for that long. I didn't want to be away from her for an hour, let alone a week.

Technically, my dad should be doing this, but he'd decided I was his very own whipping boy and I was to jump when he said jump. It had been like this for a couple of years now and I didn't know how much longer I was willing to eat his shit, especially now that I'd met the woman of my fantasies.

Jesus Christ, I was fucked.

"Why aren't you asleep?" Raquel grumbled sleepily, sliding her hand over my stomach.

I gave her a gentle squeeze. "No reason."

"You don't have to stay," she said. "I mean, I like you being here, but don't feel like you have to hang around if you don't want to."

"I'm good. Just not sleepy."

She kissed my chest. "Well, since you're up…"

Positioning herself between my legs, she ran her tongue over my Howler's tattoo, then worked her way down my body. I was rock hard the second her tongue touched my skin, but when she wrapped her gorgeous mouth around my dick, I was lost. Again.

In an effort not to embarrass myself, I hooked my hands under her arms and pulled her up my body, rolling her onto her back.

"I was enjoying that," she complained.

I grinned, kissing her. "So was I. A little too much."

"Oh," she said with the cutest fuckin' giggle I'd ever heard.

I took a second to roll on a condom, then I slipped inside of her and her laugh stopped on a gasp. "You good?" I asked.

"Holy shit, yes," she hissed out.

I held her tight and turned us both so that she was straddling my hips. "Your turn, Razzle."

She settled her hands on my chest and leaned down to kiss me. "Are you sure you're ready for this?"

"Bring it."

She raised her hips slightly, then lowered her body, impaling herself and somehow, my dick got harder. Jesus, she drove me crazy.

I slid my hands to her tits and palmed her nipples into tight buds. She dropped her head back and arched into my touch as she rode me.

I drew my knees up and thrust deeper and she gripped my arms quickening her pace. "Ori, I can't… oh, god!"

She fell across my chest as her pussy contracted around me and I rolled her onto her back and slammed into her over and over until I found my own release.

"Don't stop," she begged as I pulled out of her, so I

pressed two fingers inside of her, sliding my thumb across her clit.

"Ride my hand, baby."

She did so spectacularly and cried out my name as her cum covered my hand. I lifted my fingers to my mouth and licked her juices clean. "Jesus, fuck, baby, you taste like honey."

She chuckled. "I'll take your word for it."

"I'll be right back."

I headed to her bathroom to take care of the condom and clean up, then came back and pulled her over my chest. I couldn't get enough.

I was once again struck with how big of a problem this was.

* * *

Raquel

"I've gotta head out," Orion whispered, kissing me awake.

"What time is it?" I grumbled.

"Six."

"In the morning?" I squeaked.

He chuckled. "Yeah, Razzle, in the morning."

"Where are you going?"

"Denver."

I sighed, pulling the covers tighter over me. "When will you be back?"

"I don't know, but I'll text you."

"Okay." I yawned and nodded. "Ride safe."

"I will."

He kissed me once more, then left me to sleep, but by the time I heard the door close behind him, I was wide awake. I figured I'd get up and try and get some work done, but first, coffee.

I threw on a pair of yoga pants and a T-shirt and headed downstairs as quietly as I could. I knew Sierra had a late shift at the restaurant last night, so she'd be sleeping in today, and I was not going to be the one to wake her. She was hell on wheels when her sleep was interrupted.

I made a pot of coffee and checked my emails while it brewed. I'd missed a few from school notifying me of my grades so far. I was pulling a low B, slipping into a C, in two of my classes, and I needed to get those up, but one was chemistry and I just couldn't seem to understand it, the other was microbiology. My dad would freak if I didn't get those two grades up, and since he was paying for my education, I should probably talk to my advisor about tutoring options.

I sighed. I hated asking for help. But mostly I hated feeling stupid and science had always made me feel like an idiot. It just wasn't in my wheelhouse, but I needed to understand it in order to fully grasp how the pharmacology worked. The problem was, as soon as I felt like I comprehended one piece of it, something new would pop up and it would be Greek to me.

I pulled my phone out and texted my brother. Tristan would probably know the answers to every question in this book, not that he would give them to me, but he might help me understand some of it. He texted back immediately that he was in the middle of something and would call me when he was done. It would appear I was stuck for the moment.

I sighed. There was nothing I could do about it now, so I decided to make a cup of coffee, schmear me up a bagel and work on something a little easier.

Besides, my body was deliciously sore from our activity the night before, so I used that as an excuse not to work too hard.

Orion

*D*ENVER HAD BEEN a total waste of my fucking
time. Mostly because the shops ran like a well-oiled
machine and my presence was redundant. But Dad
was a control-freak, so I'd done my due diligence
for show, and missed out on a whole day buried in
Raquel's tight warm cunt.

Fuck me, I was tired. And pissed. And fuckin' fucked.

I backed my bike into a parking space outside of
Raquel's townhouse and walked to her door. I rang the
bell, then popped a piece of gum in my mouth to cover up

the coffee I'd downed to stay awake.

Sierra opened the door and cocked her head. "Raquel's not here."

"Ah, okay. Do you know when she'll be back?"

"She's studying, so no."

I frowned. "She can't study here?"

"Well, since Trent's not here, um no," she said, her tone one of 'duh.'

Who the fuck is Trent?

"Okay. I'll shoot her a text."

"You couldn't have done that in the first place?"

"I did. She didn't respond." I didn't know why the fuck I was explaining myself to her, it was none of her business, but I couldn't seem to help myself.

"Well, maybe you could have used that as a clue," she retorted.

"If you're done bustin' my balls, I'm gonna go ahead and leave now."

She settled her hands on her hips. "But I was just starting to have fun."

I couldn't stop a smile. "See ya later, Sierra."

"Bye, sexy."

She closed the door, and I headed to my bike. Before riding out, however, I sent Raquel another text, then made my way to the compound.

"Any issues?" Dad asked as I walked in.

"Are there ever?" I snapped.

He raised an eyebrow. "Somethin' crawl up your ass, boy?"

I fuckin' hated it when he called me 'boy.' Especially, considering he expected me to take the club over when he retired, but refused to acknowledge I was a grown ass man.

"Maybe the time I just fuckin' wasted haulin' my ass to Denver when I didn't need to."

Dad dragged his hands down his face and shook his head. "Consider this a teachable moment that you'll thank me for later."

"Yeah, whatever," I said, and walked away. I was too pissed off to get into it right now.

* * *

Raquel

I sat staring at my microbiology book, the words swimming in front of me. My tutor, Trent, was a no-show. His little brother had fallen off his bike and broken his arm, so it was all hands on deck in regards to his family. I got it. Family was everything. But it left me without a snowball's chance in hell to pass my test tomorrow. Deciding that giving up was a better choice than trying to understand that which could not be understood, I shoved my books back in my bag and made my way out of the library.

I powered up my phone as I climbed into my car and put on my seatbelt. Two texts from Orion and one missed call. My stomach fluttered with horny little butterflies, hoping he was still up as I called him back.

"Hey, Razzle," he said, answering immediately.

"Hey. Are you back already?"

"Yeah. Are you still studying?"

"How did you know I was studying?" I asked, starting my car.

"Stopped by your place. Sierra filled me in."

"You stopped by my place?"

"Yeah."

A pool of molten lava settled in my belly. He'd missed me. "On your way home?"

"Yeah."

"Adam Graves," I admonished, biting my lip. "Are

you getting attached to me?"

He chuckled. "Kinda dig your pussy, baby, but you already know that."

"It kinda digs you, too," I said.

"Yeah?"

"Yeah," I breathed out.

"Wanna swing by the cabin?" he asked.

"Is that what you call your clubhouse?"

"Yep."

"Wow, you're inviting me to the clubhouse?" I mused. "That sounds like some kind of commitment."

He laughed. "Not at all. You're at the university library, right?"

"I'm not sure I'm comfortable with you knowing that. It's kind of stalker level."

"Are you?"

I sighed. "Yes."

"Okay, it's closer to here than your place, and since I'd like to bury myself deep sooner than later, it'll take less time for you to come here, than for me to go to you."

He had a point. "Okay."

"Yeah?"

"Sure. I need a distraction, anyway."

"We'll talk about that when you get here. I'll text you the address."

"Perfect," I said.

"Are you okay?"

"Golden."

"Okay, Razzle, I'll see you soon."

We hung up and he texted me immediately. I was surprised to see the cabin was less than five miles from the University, so I followed the GPS and arrived at a large set of gates where I pressed the call button.

"What?" a gruff voice crackled through the speaker.

"Hi, um, this is Raquel. I'm here to see Orion."

A few seconds later, the gigantic gates inched open and I pulled my car through.

Wow.

Spectacular.

The main clubhouse was a ways down the road, but I could see it lit up surrounded by the mountains and it was breathtaking.

I have always loved my brother's club. The giant barn on acres and acres of Georgia land, but this...this was something otherworldly. God, I bet it looked amazing when the snow came. I suddenly hoped I'd be invited back in the winter.

I parked in front and made my way up the porch steps where I was met by Orion in the form of his mouth on mine. I gripped his cut and held on as he wrapped his arms around me and pulled me close.

"Hi," he said, breaking the kiss, but dropping his forehead to mine.

"Hi," I whispered.

He kissed me once more, then took my hand. "Come on in."

I let him lead me inside and realized immediately I'd come on a special night.

"Oh, shit, it's family night," I breathed out.

"It is."

I tugged on his hand to make him stop walking.

He faced me with a raised eyebrow. "What, Razz?"

"I think I should leave."

"Why?"

"Because we're not at family night level, Ori. It feels wrong."

He sighed. "You're family of a sort."

"But you're taking me in as your...guest. People could get the wrong idea."

"They won't. Come on."

I stared up at him for several seconds before realizing I wanted this a little more than I was willing to admit.

"Are you sure people won't think we're together?" I whispered.

"I'm sure," he whispered back.

"Okay," I said.

We headed into the great room and I removed my hand from his, which I could tell he didn't like, but I refused to be labeled as his woman.

I saw Sundance raise an eyebrow in our direction before planting a smile on his face and making his way to us. "Raquel."

"Hey, Sundance."

"Welcome."

I smiled, sliding my hands into the pockets of my jeans. "Thanks."

"Who's this?" a feminine voice asked.

I turned toward the sound, and a drop-dead gorgeous blonde approached, her blue eyes sparkling with mischief.

"Letti, this is Raquel," Orion said.

"She's Doc's sister," Sundance provided. "Dogs of Fire Prez."

"Oh, you're from Savannah," she said.

"I am. It's nice to meet you."

"It's *super* nice to meet you, too," she said in a slightly sing-song voice.

"Ignore my sister," Orion said.

"Or don't," she retorted. "I think you and I might need to get a drink."

"Violet," Orion warned.

"I think so, too," I piped in, and followed her to the bar.

"Jesus Christ," I heard Orion hiss behind us, and I bit back a smile.

"How long have you known my brother?" she asked as

we sidled up to the makeshift bar.

"A couple of weeks."

"No kidding?"

"I met him at Smiley's. Come to find out, my brother put out a word to watch over me."

"Oh, they're assholes like that, aren't they?" she complained.

I chuckled. "Very much so."

"Squeaker, shots, please," she demanded to the biker behind the bar.

He pulled out the bottle of Don Julio Añejo and two shot glasses, pouring the tequila into each, then setting the bottle on the bar beside them.

Violet lifted hers and directed me to do the same. I did and she said, "To overprotective biker brothers." Then we clinked glasses and downed the deliciousness that was high quality tequila.

"Who are you calling overprotective?" a deep voice demanded from behind me.

I turned to see yet another illegally gorgeous man, younger than Orion, but not by much I'd guess.

"Drake, meet Raquel."

He grinned. "You're Doc's sister."

"I am."

"Nice to meet you," he said, pulling me in for a bear hug.

"What the fuck are you doing, Drake?" Orion snapped, pulling me behind him.

"It's fine," I said, feeling my face heat.

Drake laughed. "I was just making Raquel feel welcomed."

"Well, you can do that without touching her," Orion ground out.

I tugged my wrist away from the vice grip of his hand holding it and tried to shrink into the floor. Violet held another shot of tequila out to me and I took it and downed it quickly.

"I'm gonna take Raquel upstairs," Orion said.

I shook my head. "No, you're not."

"Yeah, I am."

"No, that's okay," I countered.

"I think we should talk about this."

"I think we're good," I argued.

"We'll be right back," he said, and took my hand again, practically dragging me away from his family and pulling me through a door just off the kitchen. I quickly realized it was a bunkroom of sorts and looked like it was set up for younger kids with the bright bedding and Marvel movie posters.

"What are you doing?" I growled.

"I thought we had a plan," he said.

"You failed to mention it was family night and that your *entire* family was here," I pointed out. "I am not going upstairs with you when you know very well they could report back what we're doing to my brother. Nope, no way in hell."

"No one'll say a goddamn thing."

"But they'll know. I was liking this being between you and me," I said.

"So, you're *not* gonna let me bury my dick deep inside of you?" he asked, pushing me against the wall gently and leaning down to get eye level with me.

I shivered. "Not tonight, no."

"Are you sure?" He ran his tongue over my bottom lip, and I squeezed my eyes shut, taking a deep breath.

"Yes, I'm sure."

"Liar," he rasped, covering my mouth with his.

I couldn't stop myself from looping my arms around his neck and thrusting my tongue between his lips. His hands slid to my ass, squeezing gently, then lifting me so I could wrap my legs around his waist.

I'd never had someone strong enough to haul me around, and Orion did it with ease. Considering I was one hole-punch away from a free Cinnabon, my twelfth in less than a year, this was impressive.

His hands slid under my T-shirt and his nail scraped my nipple, eliciting a moan from me and driving me to distraction.

"Wait," I panted out. "We can't."

"We absolutely can," he argued, kissing me again.

"Please, Ori," I begged. "You can come to my place tomorrow night, but I just... can't do this here. Not to-night."

"Jesus," he hissed. "Fine."

I smiled, the pained expression on his face strangely ego boosting. "I'm sorry."

He adjusted his rock-hard dick and took a few deep breaths. "Give me a second and we can go back out to the great room."

I bit my lip as he walked the perimeter of the room, his hands on his head, probably thinking about baseball or something to get his erection under control. I felt for him. I was primed and ready to go myself, but I knew I was do-ing the right thing. Even if it felt like it was incredibly wrong.

After a few minutes, he faced me again, and leaned down to kiss me quickly. "Tomorrow."

"Tomorrow," I promised.

He stroked my cheek, then gave me a quick nod and led me out of the room.

Violet approached, another glass of tequila in her hand and handed it to me. "One more," she said, sounding ex-tremely cheeky.

"I think you may have had enough." Orion tried to reach for Violet's glass, but she licked it, then downed the shot with a grin.

"I licked it, it's mine," she retorted.

I took my shot, then grinned. "I should drink some water and eat something."

"I'll show you where the food is," Orion said, after snagging a bottled water from behind the bar.

"Thanks."

We walked to the tables filled with food and he handed me a plate. I noticed Violet reach for the donut on Drake's plate, but he picked it up and licked it before she could grab it.

"What's with the licking?" I asked.

Orion chuckled. "Letti and Drake started doing it when they were younger. Mostly because Letti was notorious for stealing food off other's plates. She'd say she wouldn't want anything, then eat what we got."

"I hate that," I admitted.

"We did too. Drake more than me, so he would lick everything on his plate so she wouldn't steal it. After a while, I started doing it as well, because she started pilfering from me. It's been an inside joke forever."

I grinned. "I like it."

For the rest of the night, I drank, I ate, and I found myself falling in love with another amazing group of people. It could have been the tequila, Violet was very good at making sure I never had an empty glass, but I found myself snuggling close to Orion as the night went on and loved how I fit against him like I was made for him.

"We should get you to bed," Orion whispered.

I smiled, my eyes closed, and nodded. "'K."

He stood, pulling me up beside him, and wrapping an arm around my waist. "Come on, Razzle, this way."

I honestly didn't register he was taking me up to his room until he settled me on a bed and kissed me. I grabbed his arms, the room spinning a little. "I shouldn't stay here."

"You're drunk, beautiful, so you are staying here."

"Can you drive me home?"

"I'm also a little drunk," he said. "Don't worry. I'll be a gentleman."

I nodded, then passed out.

* * *

The sound of birds singing felt more like woodpeckers attacking my skull. Not to mention, the Colorado sunshine beaming in my face. I groaned, rolling over and my face landed on a hard chest. I opened one eye and saw Orion grinning down at me.

I closed my eye again and sighed, snuggling closer to him. "What time is it?"

"Nine."

I kissed his chest.

"How ya feelin'?"

"Like—wait!" I sat up. "Nine?"

"Yeah."

"Shit!" I squeaked, throwing the covers off and noticing I was just in my panties and T-shirt. "Where are my clothes?"

"On the chair," he said, nodding toward the window. "What's wrong?"

I jumped out of bed and started dragging my clothes on. "I have my microbiology exam. In…" I glanced at the clock, "…twenty-two minutes. Shit, shit, shit!"

Orion slid out of bed and I tried to ignore the fact he was buck naked. "What do you need from me?"

"A bathroom, a toothbrush, maybe a comb, and a huge cup of coffee…to go."

He nodded to the wall behind me. "Bathroom's behind that door. There's a toothbrush and comb in there. I'll grab coffee and meet you downstairs."

"Okay," I said, and rushed through my truncated morning routine, then headed downstairs to find Orion waiting for me with a travel mug of coffee and a muffin. "Oh my god, thank you," I breathed out and made a run for my car.

I slid into my seat with barely three minutes to spare. I hoped I didn't need to pee, because the doors were about to be locked for the next two hours.

Raquel

B Y THE TIME I pulled up to the townhouse, my body and brain were mush. I practically crawled inside and up to my room, flopping onto my bed just as my cell phone buzzed. I moved just enough to take it out of my pocket and put it to my ear. "Hello."

"You sound wiped," Orion said.

"That's an understatement. I just want a hot bath and my bed."

"How about you do that, and I'll grab dinner?"

"I don't know if I'm up to a vigorous night, Ori."

He chuckled. "No pressure. I'll feed you and you can

sleep."

"Oh my god, that sounds amazing, especially if it's Chinese."

"I can make that happen, Razzle. What do you want?"

"Surprise me," I breathed out. "But I definitely want broccoli beef, broccoli chicken, and noodles."

"Anything else?"

"No, that's good. Unless you want to grab shrimp rolls."

"I can do that."

"And egg flower soup."

"I'm gonna hang up now before you order the whole restaurant."

"Okay." I smiled. "Oh, wait. Crab puffs."

"Okay, Razz, I'll get crab puffs."

"I thought you were hanging up."

"Doing that right now."

"See you soon," I said, and dropped my phone beside me on the bed.

I felt my shoes being removed and lifted my head with a groan.

"Sorry, Razz, didn't mean to wake you," Orion whispered.

"Wake me?" I rolled over and looked up at him.

"You were dead to the world when I got here."

I scrubbed my knuckles over my eyes to wipe the sand out. "When did you get here?"

"Couple of hours ago," he said. "Sierra let me in."

I sat up. "Did she eat all the food?"

Orion chuckled. "No, baby. She had to head to work."

My stomach rumbled. "Good. I'm starving."

"You finish waking up and I'll heat the food."

"Okay, thanks," I said, and took some time to put a little makeup on and brush out my hair. I also changed into something that wasn't what I wore yesterday.

Rushing downstairs, but stopping at the bottom step to take a few deep breaths and try not to look super eager to see the god that was Adam 'Orion' Graves, I smoothed my hands over my stomach and strolled into the kitchen.

I'd barely gotten across the threshold when my body was hauled against his and my mouth was kissed so thoroughly, I debated whether to skip dinner and eat him first. My stomach rumbled, making my choice for me.

"Hi," I breathed out.

"Hey," he said, grinning. "You look beautiful."

"Sleepy's your thing?"

"Everything 'you' is my thing."

I blushed. "I take it Denver went well?"

"It was a fucking waste of time, actually," he said, releasing me and setting a glass of wine and a plate piled high with food on the island.

I slid into a stool and frowned. "Is that why you're back early?"

"Partly." He leaned against the counter across from me and twisted off the top of a beer. "I didn't really need to be there, but Dad's kind of a control freak, so I had to play his game."

"You and your dad seem close. Is that not the case?"

He sighed. "It's complicated."

"How so?"

"He's got expectations about me taking over when he retires, but he refuses to let go of anything while still barking orders. Sometimes, I don't always agree with how he goes about things and we butt heads. But it's been getting worse lately, especially since we opened the stores in Denver."

"They're your stores, too, right?"

He cocked his head. "How did you know that?"

I dropped my gaze to my food. I may or may not have had Rabbit do a deep dive into Orion and his history.

Rabbit had been Doom's recruit back in the day, and he was one of my best friends.

"Raquel?" he pressed. "Did you do a background check on me?"

I shoved a bite of beef broccoli into my mouth and shrugged, chewing dramatically as he watched me through narrowed eyes.

He grinned. "Glad you did that, Razzle."

I nearly choked on a swallow. "What? I didn't."

"Means you like me. You really, really like me."

"How do you figure?"

"If you didn't, you wouldn't care to find out more about me. And since you know that there's a shit ton I can't tell you, it's flattering that you'd try to get the information illegally."

"I did nothing illegal."

His grin widened and I realized he'd just got me to admit that I did, in fact, do exactly that.

I rolled my eyes. "Don't get too cocky. I did a background check on Sierra."

"Liar."

He was right. I was a liar. In fact, he's the only person on the planet I've ever wanted to know more about, but he didn't need to know that. "Would you please stop reading my mind?"

"Nope." He grinned. "I like your mind."

I took a sip of wine and studied him. "I thought you were going to be gone for a week."

"Plans changed." He cocked his head. "How'd your test go?"

I sighed. "Terribly."

"It can't be that bad."

I raised an eyebrow. "I suck at science, Orion, it was worse than bad."

"Need some help?"

"I think it's way too late for help," I grumbled.

"I'm good at science, Razzle, so whatever you need, you let me know."

"Are you good at chemistry and microbiology?"

"Did you know that I fuck around with our plants and have created several strains that focus on different outcomes for our clients?"

I gasped. "What? No. You do?"

"Microbiology's my jam, Razz."

"Why didn't you tell me this sooner?" I complained.

"You didn't ask." He shrugged. "And it looks like that little nugget of information didn't come up on your background check."

I dropped my head in my hands. "No, it certainly did not."

"Just say the word, baby, and I'm all yours."

"Thanks. For now, though, I want to finish this delicious food and maybe fuck your brains out."

He nearly did a spit take, but recovered quickly. "I can get behind that."

"I know you can," I retorted. "You'll also be getting behind me, so you better be ready."

He pushed away from the counter and leaned toward me. "I've been ready since you denied me yesterday. I can only jack off so much before I'm raw, so I can assure you, I'm more than ready."

I set my fork down. "That sounds uncomfortable."

"It is."

"I probably shouldn't make you wait any longer, huh?"

"Probably not."

Despite the fact I hadn't finished my food, I slid off my stool, hungry for something else, and smiled. "Race ya!"

I took off for the stairs, laughing when I heard the beer bottle clank in the sink and his heavy footsteps following me. I had to stop part way up the steps because I was laughing so hard, I couldn't breathe.

This gave Orion an advantage and I found myself lifted off my feet and carried the rest of the way to my bedroom. "You're going to throw your back out."

"Shut it, woman."

"Rude," I retorted.

"Yeah, you saying bullshit like that *is* rude." He set me on my feet and slid his hand to my neck. "You're beautiful, Raquel, so shut it."

"Look, I'm not saying I'm not pretty, but I'm also self-aware enough to know I'm not the skinniest person on earth—"

He squeezed my neck. "I swear to Christ Raquel, if you finish that sentence, I'm going to gag you."

I bit my lip. "Kinky."

He smiled. "You have no idea."

I chuckled. "Hopefully, you'll show me eventually."

"We'll work into that," he promised, leaning down to kiss me quickly. "For now, though, you're gonna get naked and I'm gonna watch you do it."

"I'm wearing yoga pants and a sweatshirt, Ori. Not really good stripping material."

He sat on the edge of my bed and leaned onto his elbow. "Improvise."

I held up my finger. "Give me a second."

I shut myself into my closet and stripped really quick, then I improvised.

* * *

Orion

While Raquel was in her closet, I stripped and pulled the covers down, sitting on the edge of the mattress.

"Ready?" she asked.

"Yeah, baby, so ready."

She walked out... well, tried to sashay her way out and I bit back a laugh. She wore a white kimono adorned with pink cherry blossoms, a forest green terry cloth sash around her waist, the end of which she was twirling as she limped toward me.

I looked down and noticed she wore heels, but in the darkness, she must not have noticed that they were two different colors and also a difference in heel height.

"What are you wearing?" I asked through my laughter.

"I'll have you know, this is a very special kimono. Sierra brought it back from Japan after her senior trip."

"Where's the obi?"

"You know what an obi is?"

"I might be a biker, but I did happen to graduate top of my class," I pointed out. "So? The sash?"

"I don't know. I'm improvising, okay?" she whined, dramatically.

"And the shoes?"

"Shit. I wondered why I was lopsided." She glanced down. "I just thought I was out of practice walking in heels."

She stood looking so fucking cute, an expression of irritation covering her face and I couldn't stop myself from bursting into full on belly laughs.

"Oh, fuck it," she snapped, and threw her sex costume into the corner, then jumped into bed beside me.

I grabbed her around the waist and guided her to her back, leaning over her. "Do you know how fuckin' cute you are?"

She tugged on my beard. "You find my humiliation cute?"

"I find the fact that you are natural, honest, and stunningly beautiful, cute."

She smiled. "You make me feel beautiful, you know

that?"

I grinned, leaning down to kiss her quickly. "Good."

I slid my hand between her legs, her pussy already wet, and pressed two fingers inside of her.

"Don't make me wait, Ori," she begged.

I knelt between her legs, sliding into her slick heat, feeling her walls contract around me and I let out a groan as I buried myself to the hilt, linking our fingers together and dragging them above her head. Keeping her hands anchored to the mattress, I slammed into her harder and harder, as deep as I could, until she screamed my name and her cum covered my cock.

Jesus, there was seriously nothing better than being inside of her. Except maybe talking to her, laughing with her, and just being in her presence.

I was falling for this woman, fast.

But she was unaffected by me and I'd never been here before. I'd never had to play it cool because I'd never felt this way about anyone.

Giving one more thrust, I came inside of her, rolling us so she was wrapped around me, on our sides facing each other.

"You are perfect, baby. You know that?"

She smiled, running her thumb over my lower lip. "Good. I have you fooled."

I chuckled, kissing her one more time before cleaning up and taking her back to bed.

Raquel

Present day…

*T*HE POWER THAT *Orion's dick has over my body is probably unhealthy.*

This thought fluttered through my mind as he slammed into me from behind and I came hard and fast, like I always did.

"Fuck," he breathed out as his cock pulsed inside of me and he rolled us onto our sides, still connected, kissing the nape of my neck. "I'm kind of addicted to you, Razz."

I sighed. "Ditto."

There hadn't been a night we weren't together since our first date at Smiley's. This was a problem. Mostly because I couldn't get enough of him, and I was way behind on my thesis and research due to that fact. I'd also failed my microbiology exam and had to beg for a chance to retake the test. Not that it mattered, I was pretty sure I'd fail the retest too.

This was supposed to be a friends-with-benefits arrangement, but we couldn't seem to take a break from each other, and I was finding it overwhelming.

He slid out of me and I rolled to face him. "I need to get this thesis written."

"What's stopping you?" he challenged.

"Your dick is."

He grinned, sliding a lock of my hair behind my ear. "You're good for my ego, baby."

"I need you to do me a favor."

"Okay," he said in suspicion.

"I need you to stay away for three days. Even if I beg, you have to leave my vagina alone."

He laughed. "Not sure I can handle you begging."

I ran my finger between his pecs, tracing the Primal Howlers logo tattooed across his chest. "I know, but you have to resist my call. Can you do that?"

He frowned. "You're serious."

"As a heart attack," I ground out. "I'm failing two classes, and my research is junk right now. My dad's gonna hit the roof if I can't get these grades pulled up."

"Do you always care about what your dad thinks?"

"He's paying for my education, so abso-fucking-lutely."

"I have a feeling you'd care even if he wasn't."

"And what's wrong with that?" I snapped, sitting up and sliding off the bed. "My parents are amazing. I get that you can write your dad off with a single thought, but I can't do that to mine."

"It appears I hit a nerve." He rolled onto his back and dragged his hands down his face. "No need to get all worked up about it, Frazzle. I was just makin' an observation."

"That's *Razzle* to you."

"Not when you're this wound up, it's not," he retorted.

I let out a frustrated squeak and stomped into my bathroom.

"Are you picking a fight with me on purpose?" he asked, crossing his arms and leaning against the doorframe.

"I'm not picking a fight," I countered as I started the shower. "You're being an asshole."

"Okay, Princess, I'm being an asshole." He raised his hands in surrender. "I'll go ahead and leave now, so you don't have to deal with my assholery."

"Great. Don't call me for three days."

"Don't worry. I won't fuckin' call you at all."

With that, he turned on his heels and left and I stepped into the shower and sobbed, even if it was for the best.

* * *

Orion

I climbed on my bike and headed home, pissed off and looking for a fight. Jesus, that woman had me doin' things I never did, the least of which was letting her wrap me around her fuckin' finger. It stopped now.

Our compound was surrounded by mountains with a huge log cabin about a quarter mile from the entry gates and several smaller structures dotted throughout the landscape. I made my home in the main log cabin, along with a bunch of the younger guys. Dad had his own place, one he'd shared with my mother before she died, and my younger siblings. Since Dad and I were rubbing each other the wrong way, I decided moving into the main house would be a good idea.

Parking my bike, I headed inside the main building and found the room full of my brethren and more than a few women I'd never met. There were at least three of them currently knelt between biker's legs, sucking them off.

"Orion!" Grimace called out. "New strip club opened. Look at what it has to offer. Come join us."

Jesus, strippers and bikers. Could there be anything more cliché?

I gave him a chin lift. "Hey, brother. You have fun. I got some shit to do."

"Your loss," he grumbled, dropping his head back as the bleach blonde went to town on his dick.

I walked past the kitchen and saw my dad inside chatting up a very young redhead and drinking a beer.

"Hey, Ori," he called.

"Hey." I headed into the room and opened the fridge, grabbing a beer.

He raised an eyebrow. "You're back early."

"Yeah." I screwed off the top and took a swig.

"Everything okay?"

"Yeah," I lied.

The redhead smiled at me. "I'm Everly."

"Orion."

"Everly goes to school with your sister."

Violet had just started her junior year at UCCS, and Dad tended to keep her away from nights like tonight.

"Oh yeah? Is Letti here?"

"Yeah," Dad said, and I frowned.

"Seriously?"

"They're leaving ASAP," Dad said rather pointedly. "Right?"

"Yes," Everly confirmed, her cheeks pinkening.

"Got it!" Letti said, walking into the room and waving her phone in the air. "Oh, hey, Ori."

"Hey, sissy."

She wrapped her arms around my waist and squeezed. "I miss you, jackass."

I grinned. "Miss you too, fartface. Where are you guys goin' tonight?"

"Girls night," she said. "I left my phone here yesterday, so I had to come get it."

"No, you didn't," Dad countered. "I coulda brought it to you."

She waved her hand dismissively. "I wasn't going to make you go out of your way when it was my mistake."

"Don't think you're understanding my words, baby girl."

"Oh, I understand them perfectly," she said. "I'm just ignoring them."

"Violet," he growled.

"Daddy, I'm fine. I haven't seen anyone getting fucked from behind, my virginal eyes are safe." She rolled her eyes for my benefit and threw her phone in her purse. "Everly and I'll go out the back, so we miss the orgy."

"Jesus Christ," Dad hissed.

"I haven't heard that yelled out in ecstasy either, so my equally virginal ears are also safe."

I couldn't stop a laugh as my dad glared daggers at her.

"How's Raquel?" Violet asked. I shrugged and she frowned. "What did you do?"

I shook my head. "Nothing. It's not like we're a thing."

"But I *like* her," she whined. "She's pretty and funny and doesn't take your shit."

"Well, maybe *you* should date her, then."

48

She wrinkled her nose. "You're salty today. Did she dump you?"

I ignored her, taking a swig of beer.

Violet smiled. The one that always made me feel like she was reading my mind. I kept my expression as neutral as possible and she finally faced Dad. "I love you to the moon and back, Daddy."

He sighed. "Love you, too, baby girl."

She kissed his cheek, then guided Everly out of the kitchen and I relaxed.

"You gonna be able to make that run tomorrow?" Dad asked.

"Already told you I would."

"You *are* fuckin' salty." He raised an eyebrow. "Trouble in paradise?"

"Considering there was no paradise, there can't be trouble."

"Right. Well, have a little fun and unwind. Tomorrow's gonna start early."

I gave him a chin lift and he left me standing in the middle of the kitchen, uninterested in anything that was happening out in the great room.

Goddammit, I needed to get a fuckin' grip.

* * *

Raquel

I awoke the next morning and realized I needed a change of scenery, so I called my brother and let him know I was coming for a visit. I'd already made a reservation, so he couldn't say no, even if he wanted to.

I packed quickly and headed downstairs to find Sierra pulling muffins out of the oven. "You baked?"

"I couldn't sleep. Where are you going?"

"I'm going home for a few days. I need to get this thesis written."

She cocked her head. "Is everything okay? Why do I get the feeling this is more about one very hot biker and less about your thesis?"

"Well, my arrangement with Orion is over, so it doesn't matter either way."

"He dumped you?"

"We weren't together," I pointed out.

"What a fucking asshole," she hissed.

"Claws in, Sierra. It's for the best." I snagged a muffin out of the tin. "I was so distracted by his peen, I wasn't paying attention to my own life."

She handed me a mug and I poured coffee into it. "Well, I still say he's an asshole if you're having to run home to escape."

I smiled. "I miss my family, so it's a good excuse to see them."

"Are you okay, though?"

"I'm good, honey. I promise."

"Well, I'm gonna head to work. Text me your flight info and I'll pick you up when you get back if I can."

"Sounds good."

Sierra headed out and I ordered a car. The flight left a lot to be desired, with turbulence galore, but once I was on the ground, I started to relax. There was something about being home. I made my way out of the airport and grinned, making a run for Rabbit.

I dropped my bags and he lifted me off my feet in a bear hug. "Hey, sweetheart."

"Oh my god, I've missed you."

He chuckled, setting me back on the ground. "Back atya. Come on, I'm parked illegally."

"You always were a rebel."

We walked outside and Rabbit threw my bags in the back of Tristan's truck while I climbed inside, and then we pulled out of the airport.

"So…"

"So?" he asked, glancing at me, then focusing back on the road.

"How's Parker?"

"Fuck me," he ground out. "You gotta start in immediately, Raquel?"

I shrugged. "Well, damn. I thought for sure she'd have come around by now."

Rabbit had been in love with Parker Powers from the second she'd arrived on the scene with Willow and Jasmine. Both women were married to Dogs and I was certain Parker would fall for Rabbit to round out the group. Apparently, I was wrong.

"You and I are supposed to have a thing, remember?" he pointed out.

"Yeah, I torture Tris with the illusion of that whenever I can."

He chuckled. "Good for you."

"I'm sorry she's not seeing the brilliance that is you."

"It's all good," he said. "Plenty of fish."

Rabbit guided the truck through the giant gates at the entrance to the compound and my heart started to race, the excitement at being home palpable.

The Dogs' main meeting house was a huge antebellum tobacco barn they'd converted into private bedrooms, offices, and a meeting hall. It sat in the middle of a fenced compound on thirty acres, along with outbuildings that housed workshops and a couple of old slave quarters. The workshops were used for everything from car repair to iron works and Olivia kept threatening to renovate the slave quarters and make them actual homes. The original house had burned down in the early nineteen-hundreds and had sadly never been rebuilt.

I jumped out of the truck and rushed inside, finding

Olivia and Jasmine in the great room, laughing about something. God it was good to be home.

"Room for one more?" I asked, hugging Olivia, then, Jasmine.

"Always," Olivia said.

"Where's Tristan?" I asked.

"He's making food," she said just as my brother walked out with a plate, handing it to Olivia before hugging me.

"How was your flight?" he asked.

"It was fine," I said. "But I'm kind of tired. Do you care if I turn in?"

"Not at all," he said. "You know where you're going?"

I grinned. "Unless I can sleep in the bunny hutch, then yes."

"Jesus Christ," Doc hissed. "Go to bed. Your shit's already been taken up to your room."

"Thanks, Tris." I kissed his cheek, then hugged Olivia. "Night."

I hightailed it upstairs, hoping my brother didn't guess I was sad, and saw Rabbit leaving my room. "Your bags are inside."

"Thanks." I hugged him, holding on a little longer than usual.

"Hey, you okay?" he asked, stroking my back.

"Yes. I just missed you."

He kissed the top of my head. "Missed you too, sweetheart."

I pulled away with a smile. "I'll see you tomorrow."

"'Night."

I closed myself into my room and tried not to cry myself to sleep.

Orion

AGAINST MY BETTER judgement, I rode over to Raquel's place before my run, chastising myself for doing it, but unable to turn around.

I pulled up just as Sierra was unlocking the door. She turned and faced me, glaring daggers at me. "What do you want?"

"I want to see Raquel."

"Well, she's not here."

"When will she be back?" I asked, trying to ignore her hostile attitude.

"Oh, I don't know," she ground out. "A couple of

months, I don't know."

1at does that mean?"

.e needed a break, so she took a vacation."

w here did she go?"

"None of your fucking business."

I sighed. "Okay, babe. I get it. You're pissed about my fight with Raquel and she obviously filled you in on her version of it."

"Actually, she said nothing. You just filled me in, and now I hate you even more."

"Jesus Christ, Sierra, give me a break. Just tell me where Raquel went."

"No. Maybe if you realize you just lost the best thing to ever happen to you, you'll pull your head out of your ass. Have a nice life."

She let herself inside, and I swear I heard the lock turn with more aggression than normal.

* * *

Raquel

I awoke later than usual and stretched, relishing the feeling of being well-rested. I hadn't slept this well for months and I was once again glad I was home.

I took an extra long shower, blow dried my hair but left my face free of makeup, then dressed and headed downstairs.

"Are you hungry?" I heard my brother ask Olivia.

"I am," I announced, breezing into the room and straight for the coffee. "I smell bacon. There better be bacon."

Olivia chuckled. "It's a biker compound. Of course there's bacon."

Doc handed her a piece of toast and a cup of coffee. "Go sit down and eat this first. You need to start small."

"Thanks, baby." Olivia took a bite and gave him a quick, closed-mouth kiss, then headed into the great room and sat in the chair closest to the fireplace.

I followed, flopping onto one of the sofas just as Doom walked out of the kitchen, phone to his ear. "Yeah, Rabbit, let him in."

My focus turned to the foyer and I nearly spit my coffee out when Orion walked in.

"Orion, brother," Doom said with a grin, giving him a hug. "What the fuck are you doin' here?"

Very good question! Oh my god, my stomach roiled at the same time my vagina suddenly woke up. I could already feel the dampness beginning between my legs and I squeezed my legs shut to try and ease the ache.

God, seriously, this man and his dick were major trouble.

"Heard you had some trouble with the Spiders," Orion said, glancing my way. "Figured you might need a hand."

I frowned. What trouble with the Spiders?

"Appreciate that," Doom said. "Come on in. You remember Liv? Doc's woman?"

"Hi," Olivia said, staying put.

"And that's Raquel, Doc's sister."

I glared at Orion, then forced a smile and said, "Hi. It's nice to meet you."

His hand covered mine and my body thrummed at his touch. Jesus, I missed him.

"You too," Orion said, smiling when I dropped his hand like it was a hot poker.

The men walked away, and I couldn't stop staring at Orion. I wanted to lick him. Everywhere.

No, correction, I wanted *him* to lick *me*. Everywhere.

"Raquel?" Olivia whisper-hissed.

"Hm?"

"Oh my god," Olivia breathed out and I met her eyes.

"He's not here because of the Spiders, is he? He's here for you."

I focused back on my coffee. "I have no idea what you're talking about."

"I think you do."

"You're wrong."

"Raquel Susan Brooks, you better spill your guts right now, or I'm going straight into that kitchen and I'm going to ask Orion all about it."

"You wouldn't dare," I hissed.

She grinned in triumph.

"I hate you," I said.

"No, you don't," she countered. "You fear me, but you also adore me, so you're torn."

I tried not to laugh, but couldn't stop a snort. She had me there.

"Why is Orion here, Raquel?"

I shrugged. "I'm not sure. Entirely."

"Bullshit." She leaned forward and tapped my knee. "How long have you two been a 'thing'?"

I sighed. "Not long. It started as a friends-with-benefits kind of thing and I was good with that. I mean, let's be honest, if I hooked up with a biker, both Dad *and* Tristan would kill me. But now Ori's changing the rules. I told him I needed a break. Apparently, he didn't care."

"People who need a break from just a 'friends-with-benefits' type thing don't typically jump on a plane and go running to their big brothers."

"Well, you would know," I quipped.

She chuckled. "And I've got twins in my belly to prove it."

I grinned. "I can't wait to babysit."

"I can't *wait* for you to babysit," she said. "But quit trying to change the subject."

I rolled my eyes and sipped my coffee, saying nothing.

"Does Rabbit know you have no interest in him?" Olivia asked.

"Oh my god, Rabbit has eyes for one woman and one woman only. I could strip naked, kneel in front of him and offer to suck him off and he wouldn't care."

Olivia sighed, continuing to stare at me.

"Don't tell Tristan," Raquel said.

"About you or Rabbit?"

I shrugged. "Either. Both."

"Can't do that, Raquel. Sorry. I don't keep shit from your brother. It does not go well when I do."

"Well, can you not *offer* information, then?" I begged. "If he asks, tell him, but only if he asks."

"I'll try. No promises, though."

"Liv?" Rabbit called from the foyer.

"Yeah, bud?"

"Linda's here. She'd like a word."

She frowned. "With me?"

"Yeah."

Olivia left me and I used the distraction to escape to the kitchen for another cup of coffee. I was just walking back out to the great room when my brother stalked in.

"Raquel, my office, now," Tristan demanded, and made his way down the hall.

"Goddammit," I grumbled and followed into his office. "What can I do for you, darling brother?"

He closed the door behind me. "You and Orion."

"Me and who?"

Tristan raised an eyebrow and leaned against his desk. "You seriously trying that shit with me? It might work with Dad, but you forget who you're talking to."

I sighed, wrinkling my nose. "He and I have been seeing each other for a little while, but I broke things off."

"Why?"

"None of your business."

"Fair enough. But why's he here?"

I shrugged. "You'd have to ask him."

"I'm gonna fuckin' lose my religion if you don't start telling me the truth."

"I *don't* know why he's here. I told him I needed a break. He said okay, but now he's here, so I have no idea."

He cocked his head. "Did he know you were coming here?"

"No."

"Raquel," he warned.

"Okay, fine!" I snapped. "I didn't tell him anything, but he knows me enough to know that when I'm feeling any kind of emotion, I'm gonna go running to my big brother. You're my emotional support human."

He sighed and pulled me against him. "What's really goin' on, sissy?"

I burst into tears. "I don't know. I'm just all out of sorts right now."

"Why?"

"Maybe because I'm failing two of my classes," I growled, pulling away from him. "And I'm failing because I've been so wrapped up in Orion, I couldn't focus."

"Are you seriously failing two of your classes?"

"C in one and a C-minus in the other."

"Well, shit," he said.

"Well, shit, indeed, big brother. Do you have any idea what Daddy's going to do when he finds out?"

He rolled his eyes, releasing me. "You haven't told him?"

"No, I haven't told him!" I threw my hands in the air. "The second I do, he's gonna ship me home for good."

Someone pounded on the door, and I reached over and opened it. Orion walked in and glared at my brother. "What the fuck's goin' on?" he demanded.

"Oh, put your dick back in your pants," I snapped. "I told him everything. He's fine with it."

"Then why the hell are you crying?" he asked, at the same time Tristan said, "Not sure I said I was fine with it."

I turned to Tristan. "Can you give us a minute?"

He studied Orion for a minute too long and I groaned.

"Tris, please," I pressed.

He finally left and I crossed my arms and faced Orion. "What are you doing here?"

"Honestly? I don't know."

"Well, enjoy your stay. Savannah is renowned for their southern hospitality." I stepped to the door, but he took my arm and pulled me to him.

"Frazzle, give me a break."

"I will as soon as you start telling me the truth."

His thumb stroked the sensitive inside of my wrist. "I love you."

"What?" I squeaked.

He smiled. "You heard me."

"That wasn't the deal," I ground out.

"Oh, I'm fully aware of what the deal was, Raquel, but unfortunately, my heart no longer gives a shit."

"Well, that's a problem, because I'm probably coming home soon…permanently."

"I told you I'd help you."

"Yeah, and that went great," I said, my sarcasm at its height.

"Might I point out that you're the one who constantly comes up with distractions when I try to explain shit to you? Usually in the form of sucking me off?"

I sighed. "Your dick is my kryptonite."

"Well, I have a plan to make it all work."

I scoffed. "Right."

"You'll get my dick *and* an A."

This earned him a full-on snort. "You're high."

He chuckled. "I wish."

Pulling me to him, he leaned down and kissed me. I sighed, sliding my hands up his back and burrowing my face into his chest. "What's your plan?"

"It's better if I show you."

I wrinkled my nose. "I don't want to study this weekend."

"Not here, Frazzle." He stroked my cheek. "When we get home, I'll show you."

I nodded. "Did you really chase me here?"

"Depends on if you think that's a good thing or stalker level scary."

"Well, since I kind of love you too, it's a good thing."

"Then, hell yeah, I followed you. I'd follow you to the depths of hell to bring you back to me, baby, don't ever doubt it." He grinned. "But I'm so gonna smack your ass for running from me."

I slid my hand over his already growing erection. "You make a lot of promises."

"Have I ever broken one?"

I licked my lips. "Not so far, no."

"You gonna suck me off here, or are we gonna find somewhere private?"

"Private," I whispered, and dragged him out of my brother's office, once I saw the way was clear.

* * *

Orion

Raquel had just wrapped her lips around my cock when my phone buzzed on the nightstand.

"Ignore it," she demanded and went back to her task.

And Jesus, it was a beautiful task.

Unfortunately for me, however, my phone continued to

buzz, and I glanced at the screen. "It's your brother."

"Oh, then definitely ignore it," she growled.

"Baby, I can't. We're meeting about the Spiders shit going down."

She huffed and stared up at me. "You're gonna go in there with a raging hard-on?"

"Well…"

"Let me finish," she demanded.

I grinned down at her. "I can do that."

"Well, thank you so much, benevolent one."

She wrapped her mouth around my cock again and sucked gently, increasing the pressure of her tongue as she cupped my balls. I slid my hands into her hair and pulled gently as she worked my dick expertly with her mouth.

"I'm gonna come, baby," I warned and she gripped my ass, pulling me closer to her.

I couldn't stop my body from moving and I fucked her face until my balls tightened and I came down her throat. She swallowed every ounce, letting go of me with a satisfying smack. I dragged her to her feet and kissed her. "I promise I'll return the favor later."

"I'll hold you to it."

I headed downstairs and sat down just as Doc banged the gavel and called the meeting to order. Tonight was officers only in prep for church the next night, however, I had been invited and my plan was to sit quietly and observe. This wasn't my club, but I had offered to help, so Doc was letting me do that.

"Thanks for giving up your family time," Doc said. "I think it's time to make a plan about what to do with Sugar Bear."

"Kill him," Doom suggested.

"Slowly," Alamo added.

Doc nodded. "As much as I agree with both of you, if we do this, we'll have a spotlight the size of Oklahoma on us, and I'm not really interested in law enforcement being anymore up our asses than they already are."

"Are we gonna get to play with him a little at least?" Badger asked.

"Take a pinky, maybe?" Dash piped in and the room laughed.

"I absolutely plan to have a conversation," Doc said. "But first, we gotta find him. He's gone to ground."

"Like the pussy he is," Dash grumbled.

"No doubt. But Rabbit's got a lead and he's gonna follow that lead all the way. The bottom line? This is war, and like Minus said, it may have started in Portland, but it's gonna fuckin' end in Savannah."

Minus was the president of the Burning Saints MC in Portland, Oregon, and the Spiders were hitting them hard.

The room erupted in hoots of agreement and Doc banged the gavel for order.

"Orion, how long are you staying?" Doc asked.

I planned to stay as long as it took to make Raquel totally mine, but he didn't need to know that.

"I'm here until this shit is resolved," I said.

Doc nodded and turned back to my brothers. "Okay, we'll reconvene tomorrow once I have more information on where Sugar is. Lock your families down. Be prepared to have them here for a few days, but I want them guarded until lock down."

Doc banged the gavel. "Dismissed."

I rushed back up to Raquel's room, finding her in the shower. "I'm coming in."

She peeked her head out the shower curtain. "Hurry, I'm starting to prune."

I grinned, virtually ripping my clothes from my body, then stepping in behind her, giving her ass a smack. "Hands on the wall, Razzle."

She raised an eyebrow but did as I commanded. I

gripped her hips and kicked her legs apart gently, smiling when she understood my silent command and spread her legs further.

I tugged her hips toward me, forcing her hands to slip down the tile, and then I slid into her from behind and squeezed my eyes shut briefly. Jesus, her pussy was magnificent.

"There is no way I won't fall like this," Raquel rasped, so I pulled out and turned her to face me, kissing her gently.

"Wrap your legs around me."

She nodded and I lifted her, guiding my dick inside of her and bracing her against the wall.

"Am I too—"

"Shut it," I growled, and kissed her, twisting her nipple and feeling her pussy contract around me.

Raquel kissed me, our tongues battling for dominance as I buried myself deep, careful not to slam her too hard against the tile.

"I can't wait," she panted out.

I was close, so I twisted her nipple again and she exploded. I thrust twice more, and my balls tightened, then I came, kissing her deeply as my dick emptied itself inside of her.

"I love you, beautiful."

Her blue eyes softened as she smiled at me and stroked my cheek. "I love you, too."

"Let's get cleaned up and go find food."

"Okay, honey," she said, and we finished our shower, although we got dirty again before finally getting clean and heading downstairs.

Orion

T HE NEXT MORNING, it was time to deal with the Spiders. I let Raquel sleep and made my way with the group to the meeting place predetermined by Doc.

Rabbit had hacked into a few of the cameras around the industrial area just outside of Savannah, and he and Doc watched from their position in the back of a body shop near where Sugar Bear and some of the Spiders were holed up, while I waited with the rest of the guys for our marching orders.

When the orders came, Doom, Alamo, Rabbit, Otter, Badger, Dash, Doc, and I piled into the panel van, and drove the quarter mile to where Sugar Bear and the Spiders were hiding. Ozzy and Milky followed close behind in the Scout and we all parked on a small ridge overlooking the group of industrial buildings. The entire complex was surrounded by a cyclone fence but was otherwise unsecured.

"The plan is no one dies," Doc said. "We go in, grab Sugar Bear, and get the fuck out before anyone gets shot."

"What if the Spiders aren't too keen on your plan?" Alamo asked.

"That's what you're here for," Doc replied. "Remember. I want heavy cover fire from you, Otter, Dash, and Badger the second we're in. Doom and I will grab Sugar Bear, and Ozzy and Orion will cover the exit point where Milky will be waiting to pick us up."

Nods all around signified that everyone was ready to roll so we climbed out of the van and gathered behind the Scout.

Ozzy ran his hand gently along the rear fender of the Scout. He looked like he was about to puke, so Doc placed a hand on his shoulder.

"Send me the bill," Doc said, but I figured this was gonna be a tough one. Even I knew Ozzy had been restoring that truck for years.

Milky got out of the still running Scout and put his rig in place, making a few adjustments before giving Doc a thumbs up.

"Okay, let's go," Doc said, and the seven of us moved quietly down the ridge towards the cabinet shop, careful to stay out of sight.

Seconds later, the unmanned Scout flew down the side of the ridge, past us, barreling towards the complex. The large SUV tore through the cyclone fence like it was tissue paper and crashed into the side entrance of the shop with full force. The massive reinforced grill did its job by tearing an extra wide hole for us to fit through. Doom and Ozzy tossed several flash grenades through the opening, and moments later, we filed inside.

As soon as we were in the shop, Alamo, Badger, Dash, and Doc sprayed the interior of the building with a barrage of non-lethal, rubber riot control bullets, while the rest of us stayed behind them in tight formation.

"Holy shit, man. What the fuck?" one of the Spiders yelled out amidst the chaos, and then the sound of gunfire exploded.

Through the haze of grenade smoke, I watched Ozzy jump one of the Spiders who'd been knocked down by Alamo's shots, removing a knife from his belt before zip-tying his hands behind his back.

Another Spider took off, firing haphazardly behind him as he ran toward an office located at the opposite end of the shop floor. Badger and Dash took off after him, and Alamo and Doom split up to search for Sugar Bear, leaving Otter and me to deal with the last two Spiders on our own. One of which was curled up in the fetal position on the floor near where one of the flash grenades had detonated and was clearly concussed. Doc grabbed him by his cut and sat him up. His eyes were completely bloodshot, and he was bleeding from both ears.

"Where the fuck is Sugar Bear?" Doc asked, shaking him violently, but the guy was barely conscious.

I made a run toward the back, but was met by the Spiders President, Sugar Bear, holding Badger close, a gun to his head. Dash, Alamo, Ozzy and me raised our hands as we walked backwards toward Doc again, trying not to make any sudden moves in an effort to keep Sugar Bear calm enough not to shoot Badger.

"Doc, I mean it!" Sugar Bear, shouted. "Anyone comes toward me, I do this prick!"

The four of us fanned out. We needed to get Sugar Bear distracted somehow, but we moved slowly.

"Don't fuckin' move, Doc, or I'll blow a hole in this kid," Sugar Bear said as he continued moving toward Doc.

"I heard you," Doc replied, calmly.

"Doc, I don't see you lowering that gun," he barked back.

"I will," Doc replied, and kept the rifle leveled at him.

"Is Doc short for Doc Holiday or somethin'? You fancy yourself a real-life sharp-shootin' cowboy? You think you can hit me from over there without putting a bullet into your guy as well?"

"Nope."

"Then drop the rifle," Sugar Bear growled.

"I will."

"You think I'm fuckin' around here, Doc? I said put your gun down or I'm gonna shoot this fucking—"

Sugar Bear moved the barrel of his gun slightly away from Badger as he yelled, and Doc unloaded. Both Sugar Bear and Badger hit the ground from the force of the rubber bullets and Dash, Alamo, and Ozzy dogpiled Sugar Bear while Doc went to Badger. I raised my rifle in case anyone else felt the need to interfere.

"You...fucking...shot me. Ow, oh...shit," Badger said, clutching his side.

"Sorry, man, but I knew he wouldn't be expecting me to fire. I tried my best not to hit you."

"Try harder next time, will ya? I think you hit me twice."

"Looks like three from my count," Doc said as he gave Badger the once over.

The Dogs got Sugar Bear to his knees after restraining him and Doc pulled out a black hood from his inside cut pocket.

"You should have never fucked with our families, Sugar," Doc said before placing the bag over his head and turning to Dash, Doom, Alamo and me. "You guys help Badger, and Ozzy and I'll take Sugar Bear. Milky should be out back with the van by now."

We exited the building, and Doc threw Sugar Bear into the van, before sliding the door closed and yelling, "Drive!"

Milky floored it but didn't get far.

A loud pop echoed in the van and Milky's body lurched forward and he spit up blood all over the inside of the windshield. The van violently swerved as Doc struggled for the gun, punching wildly at Sugar Bear's hooded head, until he stopped moving entirely.

"Jesus Christ, Milky!" Doom shouted, grabbing the wheel from the passenger seat before reaching over with his left foot and hitting the brake.

The van came to a stop and Doc yelled to Alamo, "Watch Sugar Bear, I need to check on Milky," before getting out of the van. I could hear sirens approaching from the distance and knew we had to get the hell out of here fast.

Doc opened the driver's side door and swore. "We have to get him to the clinic right away."

"Shouldn't we take him to the fucking hospital?" Doom asked as Doc examined the wound.

"It looks like the bullet went clean through his right side and missed his liver and kidney. I'll know as soon as I get him on my table. If I can't handle it myself, we'll take him to County Hospital. Help me move him into the back."

We quickly transferred Milky into the back and Doom sped off toward the compound.

Raquel

I paced the downstairs waiting for my brother and my man to get back from putting into motion whatever hairbrained scheme they'd come up with. To say I was pissed was an understatement, and to say I was terrified was beyond. Orion had said *nothing* to me about this. He didn't even wake me this morning to say goodbye.

"Raquel, come sit down," Olivia said.

"No."

Doc walked in with a bloody Milky and all hell broke loose, but I was too busy staring at the blood on Orion to worry about anyone else. I made a run for him.

"What happened?" I demanded.

He grabbed my wandering hands. "It's not my blood, Frazzle."

I tugged his T-shirt up, trying to investigate his body.

"Baby, seriously, it's not mine," Orion said.

I fell against him and he wrapped his arms around me.

"Upstairs, right now," I growled.

"Baby—"

"I swear to god, Adam, get your ass upstairs." I pointed to the stairs. "Now."

He raised an eyebrow and I thought he might argue with me, but then he smiled and headed toward our bedroom. I followed, closing us in and finding myself lifted off my feet and dropped gently on the bed. Orion's hand landed on my ass with a hard smack and I let out a squeak. Lord, it made me so horny.

"You gonna continue to give me shit?" he challenged.

"If I do, will I get more of that?"

"No."

I wrinkled my nose. "Oh, well, then I won't give you shit."

He grinned down at me, his hands on either side of my hips. "In all seriousness, though, I need you to keep your tongue leashed in front of the guys, Raquel."

I leaned back and frowned. "Excuse me?"

He moved in to kiss me, but I covered his mouth with my hand.

"Razz."

"Repeat what you just said."

"You heard me."

I shoved his face away. "Get off me."

"Babe."

"If you don't want your dick ripped from your body, you'll get off of me immediately."

He sighed and stood, and I scrambled off the bed.

"Where are you going?" he asked.

"I'm going to ask my sister-in-law how to be a demure biker's woman who only speaks when she's spoken to," I hissed.

"Jesus, Frazzle, that's not what I'm saying."

I was no longer listening. I slammed the door closed and rushed downstairs. Unfortunately, Olivia was helping my brother patch Milky up.

"Why do you look like you're on the rampage?" Rabbit asked as he walked past me in the hall.

"No reason."

He chuckled, taking my hand and pulling me into the kitchen. "Spit it out."

"I don't think you're the right person to talk about this with."

"Why not?"

"Because you have a dick."

"Thanks for noticing." He grabbed a beer from the fridge. "Spit it out, Raquel. You know I'm a good listener."

"Oh, I can't talk to you, buddy. I am not allowed to

speak directly to you, sir. Us women shouldn't speak our minds to the 'menfolk.'"

He raised an eyebrow, but didn't say anything, and I unloaded on him, probably telling him way too much.

"Olivia would *never* let Doc get away with that shit," I hissed.

"At the risk of pissing you off further, Doc is Prez, Raquel. Orion isn't."

"Why the fuck does that make a difference?"

"Orion's low on the totem pole, sweetheart. He's got more to prove. You're also new…you know, as a couple. Doc and Olivia have been together for years. Not to mention, they've been to hell and back a few times. They've fought for their place in the world together, and Olivia's earned her stripes, so to speak."

"You're just as low as he is," I pointed out.

"Yep, which is why I know what I'm talking about."

"Is this why Parker's playing hard to get?"

"I'm done with this conversation," he ground out.

I sighed. "Sorry, I know that's a touchy subject."

"You good?"

I nodded. "Don't be mad, okay?"

"I'm not mad."

I wrapped my arms around his waist. "Then, relax."

He chuckled and hugged me. "I'm good, Raquel."

"What the fuck is going on?" Orion demanded.

I tried to pull away from Rabbit, but he held firm.

"What does it look like?" Rabbit asked. "Raquel's finding comfort in the arms of a real man."

"Rabbit," I growled.

"Oh, yeah? Why is she here with you then?" Orion retorted.

"Hopefully, he went to hell, which is where both of you macho assholes should go."

I tried to pull away from Rabbit again, but he held

firm.

"Rabbit," I snapped, just as Parker walked into the room.

Hurt flared in her eyes and she turned on her heel and rushed out the door.

"Parker!" Rabbit called, but she didn't respond. He gave me another squeeze, then released me. "You good?"

"I'm good," I assured him, and he grinned, knowing exactly what he'd done, then walked out of the room, and I guessed he went looking for Parker.

Orion crossed his arms and studied me.

"He's my friend, nothing more," I said, mimicking his stance.

"I know."

"Then why are you all stabby?"

He raised an eyebrow. "Don't like walking into a room and finding my woman in another man's arms."

"Well, don't be a douche and it won't happen."

"Baby, I wasn't trying to be a douche."

"And?"

"And, what?" he asked.

"I'm sorry for acting like a douche, even though I wasn't trying to be one," I prompted, waving my hand in a circle.

He grinned. "I appreciate your apology, but for the record, I would never call you a douche."

I threw my hands in the air and walked out of the room. I just couldn't deal with him being a dick, however, I didn't get far. Strong arms wrapped around my waist from behind and I was pulled up against Orion's chest. "Stop, Frazzle. I'm just messin' with you."

"I'm not in the mood."

"Yeah, I'm pickin' up on that." He turned me to face him and cupped my cheek. "Talk to me."

"I'm afraid this is never going to work."

"Why, baby?"

"Because I can't be what you need," I whispered.

"Jesus Christ, how did we get here?"

"I'm mouthy, Orion, in case you haven't noticed, and I'm not good at keeping my opinions to myself."

"I'm not asking you to."

"Bullshit," I hissed.

"Baby, I'm not. I love all of your opinions."

"When they're voiced in private."

He sighed. "I'm just asking that maybe you take it easy on me in front of my brothers. At least, when it's on a serious note. When I'm with my club, everything's amplified. Fighting, fucking—"

"You fuck your brothers?" I asked.

He rolled his eyes. "My club watches me closer than most. You know I'm expected to take over when Dad decides to give up his patch."

"Oh, I'm aware," I ground out.

"So, can you give me a break?"

"Can you pull the rod from your ass for five minutes?"

"I can try."

I wrinkled my nose. "Fine, then I'll try, too."

He kissed me. "I love you."

"I love you, too, but we need to set some ground rules going forward."

"What kind of rules?"

"The kind that don't involve you getting up before me without telling me what the fuck you're doing, particularly if that something is dangerous," I hissed.

"Right."

"Among others."

He cocked his head. "What others?"

"The ones I'll make up as we go along."

He laughed. "Okay, Razzle, we'll cross that bridge when we get to it."

"There might be more than one bridge."

"We'll cross those, too." He wrapped his arms around me. "For what it's worth, I missed you today."

"Well, imagine what that would feel like wondering if I was going to live or not."

"Point taken, Raquel. I heard you the first hundred times you mentioned it."

"Don't get stabby with me, Orion. This is on you."

"Baby, I've apolog—"

"You haven't actually," I pointed out.

"I have."

"You haven't."

"Okay." He sighed, dropping his forehead to mine. "I'm sorry, baby. I will do my best in the future not to worry you."

"You'll do your best in the future to tell me everything that's going on, so I don't worry."

"Nope, that's not even on the table."

I gripped his cut. "Shit."

He chuckled. "You're gettin' it."

"I can't be left completely in the dark, Ori. I'll go mad."

"I don't plan to leave you completely in the dark, baby. I promise."

I nodded, dropping my face into his chest as he wrapped his arms around me again. "I'm going to hold you to that."

He gave me a squeeze. "Wouldn't expect anything less."

I met his eyes. "Now, can we go back upstairs so you can finish what we started."

He nodded, kissing me gently, then leading me back up to our bedroom and smacking my ass as we walked inside.

Raquel

TWO DAYS LATER, we'd booked our flights home for the next day, so I decided to do a last-minute load of laundry, switching it from the washer to the dryer just as I heard the deep, bellowy voice of my dad.

"Raquel Susan Brooks, where the hell are you?"

"He's early," Tristan said, peeking into the laundry room. "Sorry, sissy. Dad's on his way. CorBran are coming, too."

"What about Mom?" I asked.

"Your mom's at your aunt's for a few days."

"So, no buffer there," I grumbled.

"Sorry, not sorry."

"Seriously, Tristan? I will get you for this," I threatened. My brother grinned and walked away in response. "And it's BranWin, not CorBran," I corrected.

"Raquel!" Dad bellowed again.

"I'm here, Daddy," I said, and walked out to the great room and straight into his arms.

"You fly home and don't call? What's up with that, Chickpea?"

"Sorry. It's been a crazy couple of days."

Brando rushed me, lifting me off my feet.

"Oh my god!" I squeaked. "Have you grown again? Lordy, you get taller every time I see you. And why haven't you returned my texts?"

Brando chuckled, setting me on my feet again. "Because I'm not a twelve year old girl."

Corwin pulled me in for a more demure hug. "Hey, sissy."

"Hey, Winnie. You look like you're bulking up."

He grinned, flexing a bicep. "Workin' on it."

"Raquel, have you seen my—?" Orion stopped mid-sentence as he walked into the room.

I pulled away from my brother and smiled. "Dad, BranWin, this is Orion. Orion, Dad and my brothers Brando and Corwin."

My dad raised an eyebrow before facing Orion and shaking his hand.

"Beer?" Tristan asked Dad, offering him a bottle.

"Thanks," he said, taking the beer, but studying me.

"Orion and I are a thing," I said.

"A thing?" Dad and Orion said, in stereo.

"I think you and I need to talk," Dad said, and I sighed.

"You can use my office," Tristan offered.

"Fine," I said, and headed down the hall. I glanced

back at Orion hoping he'd leave me alone for the moment. He crossed his arms and watched us walk back but didn't make a move to follow.

Dad stepped in behind me and closed the door, waving to a seat next to Tristan's desk. I sat down and he took the chair opposite me, setting his beer on the desk and leaning forward, his elbows to his knees. This was his 'I need to have a serious talk with you' stance.

And I suddenly felt like a child all over again.

"What's this about Cs in two of your classes?" he asked.

I forced myself not to react, but I was angry and nervous at the same time. "I haven't gotten my final grades, so those will go up."

"And who's this Orion character?"

I bit my lip. "I think he quite possibly might be the love of my life."

Dad sat back with a sigh. "I see."

I dropped my eyes to my hands, unable to look at the disappointment in my father's eyes.

"This is why you're failing."

"I'm not failing," I countered.

He raised an eyebrow.

"I'm not," I said. "And it has nothing to do with Orion. It's more about the fact that I suck at science."

"One more semester," he said. "You don't get your grades up, I'm pulling the plug. Finance-wise…I'd never pull the plug on you."

I couldn't stop a groan. My dad was a total dork.

"You can do this, chickpea," he encouraged.

"I'm going to try," I said, finally meeting his eyes again. "I've lined up tutoring."

"That's my girl."

"Did you really need to come down here and give me a lecture, though?"

"I didn't lecture, Raquel. If I give you a lecture, you'll know it."

I rolled my eyes. "Well, there is that."

He grinned. "Come on, chickpea. I need to interrogate your young man."

"No. Absolutely not."

He stood, grabbing his beer off the desk and walking out.

"Dad!" I growled, following and slamming into the brick wall that was Orion.

"I got you," he said with a chuckle.

I gripped his cut. "Where's my dad?"

"I don't know. I was takin' a piss."

"Thanks for the info."

He grinned. "You okay?"

I sighed. "Yeah. He was actually kind of cool about everything. I have one more term to pull my grades up before he cuts the money off."

Orion waggled his eyebrows. "Wow."

I nodded. "He wants to grill you ruthlessly, though."

"Let's go."

"We don't have to. We can go back up to my room and do other things."

"I'm not hiding from your dad like a pussy."

I gripped his cut. "I wouldn't think less of you if you did."

He cocked his head. "*I'd* think less of me. Come on, Frazzle, let's go face the music."

"Why couldn't I fall in love with a man who does what I tell him to?"

Orion laughed and took my hand, tugging me back out to the great room.

* * *

"We're here, baby," Orion whispered, kissing me gently.

I blinked my eyes open and smiled. "How did I not notice?"

"You're not a morning person, so the flight nearly killed you."

I chuckled. "Might be a little melodramatic."

"I believe I just quoted you warmly and accurately," he said, unbuckling my seatbelt.

Moses had picked us up from the airport and brought us back to the cabin, but he was nowhere to be seen now.

"Where's Moses?"

"He had 'shit to do,'" Orion said. "You want me to carry you inside?"

"Oh my god, crazy man, no way in hell."

He grinned and stepped back so I could climb out of the truck.

"You good to stay here tonight?" he asked. "I can take you home tomorrow."

"I've got class tomorrow."

"I can drop you at school, then pick you up."

"Me staying here on a school night did not go well last time," I pointed out.

He grinned. "I'll make sure you don't drink much, and I'll set my alarm."

I nodded. "Okay."

"Yeah?"

"Yes."

"I'm gonna fuck you," he warned.

"Yeah, I picked up on that." I smiled up at him. "I'm all in, honey."

"Good." Taking my hand, he lifted it to his lips and kissed the palm. "Come on. Let's go find some food."

"I'm dying for coffee."

"We'll get coffee too."

I followed him inside and we found the great room packed.

"Orion, my boy!" a large, bearded biker bellowed, jogging toward us. "How was your trip?"

"It was good, Wrath," he said. "The threat's been taken care of."

Wrath squeezed Orion's shoulder. "Next time you take off without warning, I'm gonna fuckin' brain you."

"Right. Sorry, brother."

"Ori?" Sundance called from the mouth of one of the hallways. "A word?"

Orion gave him a chin lift. "Be right there." He turned to me and smiled. "Be right back. Make yourself at home."

I nodded. "Just remind me where the kitchen is, and I'll make coffee."

He pointed to my right. "Through that door."

I made my way to the kitchen while Orion went to talk to his father.

* * *

Orion

"What the fuck is going through your head, boy?" my father bellowed the second his office door was shut.

"Good morning to you, too, Pops," I said, preparing myself for the torrent of criticism that was about to come.

"Why the hell did you take off without checking out?"

"Wrath already read me the riot act, okay? So, if all you're gonna do is chew my ass out about safety protocols, I really don't have time," I said, pointing a thumb to the door.

Wrath was barely five years older than me, but he was my road captain, so I should have checked in with him at the very least.

"What the hell did you say to me, boy?"

"Enough with calling me 'boy,' already," I said, dragging my hand down my face. "Jesus Christ, Dad, I'm twenty-six years old."

"Listen here, you disrespectful little shit. I've been calling you boy since you were in your mother's belly," he fumed. "Before we even knew you *were* a boy. Hell, as far as I know, you were a girl until I *willed* you into becoming a boy."

Dad was clearly in no mood for my backtalk, and I knew him well enough to detect something else had already been bothering him since before I'd even walked into the room.

"I'm sorry," I ground out. "It's just that I've told you over and over that you have to start treating me like a man."

"I will when—"

"You start acting like one," I mimicked.

"See? That's the kind of snot-nosed shit I'm talking about right there. You've been in here for less than two minutes and all you've done is run your mouth and sass me."

"As soon as I walked in, you started laying into me about not checking out, and I told you Wrath already talked to me about it. What the hell more do you want from me?"

My father's face fell. "A hell of a lot more than you're giving me, Ori. But I guess both of us are gonna be disappointed today."

He was right. I was being disrespectful to him, both as a father and as the club's president, and I felt like shit for that. On the other hand, I was pissed at him for the lack of respect he constantly showed me. "Look, I'm sorry for not checking out," I said.

"I don't want you to be sorry, Orion. I want you to do better. I need you to set an example to the younger members and the recruits. You're gonna be their president one day and I want you to have already earned their respect."

"Jesus, Dad. This shit again?"

He scowled. "The club and your future presidency is shit talk to you?"

"That's not what I meant," I said defensively before stopping and taking a deep breath, reaching for a calmer tone. "I hear you about the disrespect and you're right. But if you continually treat me like a teenager, I'm gonna act like one."

"Fair enough," my father said before sitting down behind his desk. He motioned me towards the only other chair in his office and I sat. My father hated meetings. Outside of church, which he always kept as brief as possible, his conferences were always one-on-one. He believed in keeping the flow of information tight. It was one of the few things he and I agreed on.

"Look, it's not that I don't take the president's patch seriously. It's the exact opposite. It's a big fucking deal. Especially when your old man is the club's founder and president."

"If you understand what the presidency means so well, then why don't you want it?"

In all the times my father had talked about handing his patch down to me, I'd never detected a hint of urgency, until now.

"I didn't say I didn't want it, only that I don't know right now. If I do take the patch it'll be because it's my choice to take it, not because I feel obligated to take it. Becoming president would have to be my decision and mine alone."

"No decision belongs to you alone," Dad countered. "Every decision you make affects other people. Sometimes in ways you can predict, but oftentimes, not. That's the first thing you need to know about being president."

I threw my hands up. "You're a broken record," I said

with an exasperated smile.

"I'm also coming up to the end of side B," he said in a tone that reached right through me and grabbed ahold of my spine.

"You're not *that* old," I replied, trying to ignore the fist.

"The kind of cancer I got don't especially care about that," he said and the fist in my chest squeezed.

"What the fuck are you talking about?"

"Acute myelogenous leukemia. It's aggressive and most patients don't survive once it spreads to the organs," my father said plainly. "Which it has."

"Jesus, Dad. How long have you known about this?"

"Not long. Maybe a month."

"A month! And I'm just hearing about this now?"

"Sure, we can make this all about you if that's what you need."

"Save the martyr shit. You should have fuckin' told me about this right away," I snapped.

"Well, now you know," he replied matter-of-factly. "Not that it changes anything."

"What the hell is that supposed to mean?"

"What does it matter if I die if you're not gonna take my patch?"

"Holy shit! You're unbelievable," I exclaimed. "First of all, the topic of whether or not I will ever wear the president's patch is hereby tabled indefinitely."

"Careful, you sound like you're leadin' church."

"Secondly, you're not fuckin' dying," I said flatly. "There's shit the doctors can still do, right?"

"I started chemo last week."

"You fuckin' started chemo and didn't tell me?"

"My oncologist said chemo had to start immediately."

"What about a bone marrow transplant?" I asked.

"He doesn't think a bone marrow transplant will work

at this stage, so we have to start there."

"I need you to give me your doctor's name and number and you need to tell me everything he's told you in the past month."

He pulled out his wallet and handed me a card, then leaned back in his chair. "The Apex Predators are coming for us, Ori. I can't deal with them and chemo. I need you to step up."

The Apex Predators were trying to horn in on our pot business. They'd been too slow to get the necessary grow permits and rather than do it legally, they figured they could muscle us out of ours. We weren't ones to be muscled, however, so the fuckers were shit out of luck.

"I hear you, Dad. I'm here. You've got your officers, too. You know Moses and Rocky are already on top of it."

"Yeah, I know."

I leaned forward, settling my elbows on his desk. "We got this, Dad."

"Don't get cocky, son. That's when things go to shit."

"I'm not cocky. I'm confident. I get that we need to proceed carefully."

Dad dragged his hands down his face. "I've put a call into Hatch in Portland in case we need back up."

"Hopefully we won't."

Dad nodded and I took my opportunity to cut the meeting off. "I'm gonna go check on Raquel."

"Okay. We'll talk later."

"Sounds good."

I slid the doctor's contact card into my pocket and walked out of the room.

Raquel

I FOUND THE coffee and put a pot on, then rummaged around for a mug. It wasn't hard to find. The kitchen was set up very similarly to the kitchen at the Dogs of Fire compound, which was super logical.

"Can I help you?"

I turned to the sound of the feminine voice and smiled. "Hi. I'm Raquel. I'm here with Orion, but he's meeting with his dad, so he told me to make myself at home. Do you want some coffee?"

She studied me. "No, I don't want coffee."

The woman was blonde, obviously from a bottle, and

she wore a shit ton of makeup that made her look older than she probably was. Her mouth was in an I-just-sucked-on-a-lemon pucker, and I couldn't stop myself from straightening my shoulders for some reason.

"Why are you here?" she asked.

"I'm sorry?"

She crossed her arms. "What do you want with Orion?"

"I'm not sure that's any of your business."

"Well, considering I'm fucking him, I think it *is* my business."

I narrowed my eyes. "I'm guessing you might have been fucking him at one point, but I highly doubt you are now."

"Bitch—"

"Sonja," Orion said as he walked in. "You're here early. Need somethin'?"

She smiled a sick, saccharine smile and sauntered to him, running a finger down his chest. "No, baby, I'm good."

He grabbed her hand and pushed it away. "Not sure what the fuck you're doin', woman, but you touch me like that again, and you'll be banned."

"That's not what you were saying two weeks ago."

"Oh yeah? What was I saying two weeks ago, Sonja?" Orion hissed.

"You know, when we were fucking."

"Are you high?" he snapped and headed for the kitchen door. "Aero!"

"Yeah?" Aero walked into the kitchen and I assumed he was a new recruit. I saw he had 'PROSPECT' on his cut, plus, he looked young. Like teenage young, so he was probably low on the totem pole.

"Sonja's out," Orion said.

Sonja gasped. "What the hell? You can't do that."

"I just did." Orion waved his hand. "Don't let the door hit you on the ass on the way out."

"You're a fucking liar," she snapped. "I'm taking this to Sundance."

"Try it," Orion said.

"I will." She jabbed a finger toward me. "This bitch is totally fucking you up. Everyone's talking about it, and I can see now she's obviously leading you around by the dick."

I bit back a response, fisting my hands at my side.

"Get gone," Orion growled.

Sonja stomped out of the room, and Orion gave Aero a chin lift to follow.

The recruit rushed after her and Orion turned to me. "You okay?"

"What did she mean by everyone was talking about me fucking you up?"

"Nothing. She was messing with your head."

He reached for me, but I eluded his touch.

"She's obviously a desperately pathetic cuntwaffle, but—"

He chuckled. "You're sexy when you channel your inner biker woman."

I rolled my eyes. "What did your dad want to talk to you about?" I asked.

"Nothing you need to worry about."

I sighed. "I am not going to be the thing that comes between you and your club."

"You're not. Not even close."

I bit my lip. "I don't think you're telling me the whole story."

"Baby, will you let me hold you?"

"Not right now," I said.

He crossed his arms and leaned against the kitchen island. "Don't spiral."

"Don't tell me how to feel."

"Sonja's a patch whore," he said. "She's no one."

I frowned. "I need you not to manage me right now, Orion. If she was no one, she wouldn't be here. If she didn't have something to offer, you guys would have gotten rid of her a long time ago. She may just be gash, but she's not throw away gash."

"Raquel, I did not fuck her two weeks ago."

"I know that." I waved my hand dismissively. "I'm not concerned about you and your fidelity to me. This is way bigger than us."

"Bullshit."

"How so?"

"None of this has anything to do with us," he said.

"Honey, this has everything to do with us, if 'us' means you're fractured with your club."

"I'm not fractured with my club."

I raised an eyebrow, not entirely convinced what he said was true.

"I'm not. Things are a little complicated right now, but nothing is close to being fractured."

"I can't be the reason—"

"Stop," he growled. "You are the best thing that's ever happened to me, Razzle. You will never be anything but a positive part of my life."

"Your dad looked pissed."

Orion stepped closer to me. "Not at you."

I tried to step back, but the counter stopped me, which gave Orion the chance to box me in. "Promise me that you'll tell me if I'm making things difficult for you."

He shook his head. "No."

I gripped his cut. "Why the hell not?"

"Because you and the club are separate."

"We aren't."

"How do you figure?"

"Do you want to have this conversation here?" I asked. "In public?"

He sighed. "Probably not."

I studied his face. "What's going on, Ori? The truth."

He took my hand and led me into the walk-in pantry, turning on the light and closing the door behind us. "My dad has cancer."

"Oh my god, honey, are you okay?"

"No. I'm fuckin' pissed. He's known for a month and didn't tell us."

"What does his doctor say?"

"It's bad, Raquel. Really bad. He started chemo this week. Alone."

"He didn't tell you about it?"

Orion shook his head. "Wrath dropped him and picked him up from his treatments."

I wrapped my arms around his waist. "I'm so sorry."

"Thanks, Razz. We're working it out, but things aren't good right now."

"Did he say why he didn't tell you?"

Orion shook his head. "But he didn't need to. I know why."

"You do?" I met his tortured eyes. "Do you want to share?"

"Not right now, honestly."

"Tell me later?"

He dropped his forehead to mine. "Yeah, baby. Later."

"Okay, well, I need coffee, so let's put a pin in it and we can talk about it when we're alone."

"You don't need to talk about the Sonja shit?"

"Nope," I said.

"I need you not to shut down on me."

"I'm not. I'm simply trying to be a good, subservient biker's woman and keep my opinions to myself until we're in private."

He chuckled, leaning down to kiss me. "So, you *can* be taught."

"I'm gonna teach you a few things later, Señor Douche Canoe."

Orion grinned kissing me again. "Can't wait."

"Coffee."

"Coffee." He nodded, opening the pantry door. "Are you hungry? Do you want bacon?"

"Is there ever a time someone might say they *don't* want bacon?"

"Can't think of one, no."

"Then, yes. Get to cooking DC."

He grinned kissing me again, and then he got to cooking.

* * *

The distant sound of groaning woke me, and I blinked my eyes open as I reached for Orion. He hissed and sat straight up. "Ori?"

"Fuck," he whispered.

I glanced at the clock. Two a.m. "Are you okay?"

He slid off the bed and headed to the bathroom without responding. I followed.

"Baby, you're scaring me."

"I'm okay, Raquel. It was just a bad dream," he said, turning on the faucet and washing his face.

I leaned against the doorframe. "Do you have night terrors a lot? Because, that's what this was."

"It's fine," he countered.

"Honey, it's not fine if it's continual. This was way more than a bad dream."

"They're not continual."

"Do you want to talk about it?"

"No."

"Are you sure?" I pressed.

"Raquel, I'm tired as shit. Will you drop it?"

"Sure."

"Will you drop it and not be mad about dropping it?" he challenged as he dried his face.

He knew me way too well. "Maybe."

Dropping the towel on the counter, he closed the distance between us, sliding his hands to my waist. "You are a pain in the ass."

"Would you like me to leave?" I challenged as his hands went to my butt and squeezed.

"No. I happen to love that you're a pain in the ass," he said, leaning down to kiss me.

"Are you trying to distract me?" I asked, in between kisses as he backed me out of the bathroom and toward the bed.

"Is it working?"

"Am I still talking?"

He chuckled, lifting me onto the mattress and tugging me to the edge. "When aren't you talking?"

"Are you trying to fuck me or piss me off?"

Orion grinned. "Both."

"Well, you're getting one of those right," I retorted.

He dragged my panties down my hips and the cold breeze of the air-conditioner hit my soaked pussy making me shiver. Deliciously. He slid a finger inside of me and braced his other arm on the bed next to me. "Love how wet you are for me."

"You're so fucking cocky."

He slid another finger inside of me and I arched into his hand and he pumped into me, his palm slapping me against my clit. I pressed my foot to his shoulder and used his body as an anchor to arch harder into his hand.

"Jesus Christ," he hissed, removing his fingers and hovering over me. "You're so fucking beautiful."

I licked my lips, reaching up to stroke his cheek. "Are

you going to finally fuck me or continue to piss me off?"

He chuckled. "On your knees."

I scrambled onto all fours and he slid into me from behind, giving my ass a gentle slap.

"Yes," I whispered.

"You wanna keep bustin' my chops?"

"I don't know," I retorted. "Can you fuck me correctly now?"

He buried himself deep. "Like this?"

I groaned. "God, yes. Just like that."

He gripped my hips. "Or, do you like it like this?"

He shifted slightly and when he thrust in again, his dick hit my G-spot and I exploded around him. He continued to slam into me until he built me up again and I fell flat as my pussy contracted around his dick. He was right behind me and continued to bury himself deep, grinding my clit to the mattress which built yet another orgasm in me.

I screamed into a pillow as I came apart, Orion's cock pulsing inside of me as we both found release.

He rolled us onto our sides and kissed the nape of my neck. "I love you."

I smiled. "I love you, too."

He pulled out of me, stepping into the bathroom and returning quickly with a warm washcloth. After cleaning me up, he threw the washcloth into the corner and pulled me up against him, wrapping the sheet around us. "My mom was killed by a drunk driver ten years ago."

I stilled, sliding my hand over his belly. "I'm sorry, honey."

"Dad was on a run. Checking on a couple of the shops and couldn't get back in time to see her before she took her last breath. It ripped him apart. I think it's still ripping him apart."

I blinked back tears, kissing his chest.

"He blames himself for not being here," Orion continued. "They were tight. Loved each other like crazy, but they'd had a fight before he left. She didn't want him to go for some reason. I'm not entirely sure why, but Dad has always felt he was responsible for her death."

"Do you?"

"Of course not. It was the fucking asshole who drove blitzed out of his head. But it left Dad alone with three kids and Mom had been the glue, so things fractured a little. Don't get me wrong, Dad's always been a great dad, but he broke when she died and now he's sick and I honestly don't know if he has the will to fight this."

I settled my chin on my hand and met his eyes. "You don't really think your dad will let this beat him, do you?"

Orion scrubbed his hand down his face. "I honestly don't know."

I sat up. "Have you been dealing with this all day?"

"In regards to what exactly?"

"The emotional upheaval of knowing your dad's sick and not sure if he loves you enough to fight for his life."

"Jesus Christ, Raquel, you freak me the fuck out."

"Because I know you?"

"Yeah," he whispered, and I inched toward him on my knees.

Leaning down, I kissed his belly, then straddled his hips and flattened my palms on his chest. "I'm really sorry you're dealing with this crap."

His hands slid to my hips and over my butt. "Thanks, baby."

"Can I do anything for you?"

"You're doing it." He flipped me so I was on my back and his dick was pressing against my entrance.

For the next hour, he distracted me thoroughly and I passed out wrapped around my gorgeous man.

Raquel

T HE NEXT MORNING, Orion dropped me at school with the promise to pick me up when classes were done. Only, it wasn't Orion who retrieved me. It was Sundance.

"Hey," I said, climbing into the cab of a shiny, black Ford F-150.

"Hey," he said.

"Where's Orion?"

"He's on a run."

"Oh. Okay," I said, and faced him. "I could have grabbed a ride share or called my roommate."

"I'm aware. But Orion didn't want you to do that, so I offered to come get you."

"You didn't want to send a recruit?"

He smiled, shifting the truck into gear. "Figured with the daggers you were shooting me earlier, you might need to get something off your mind."

Lordy, like father like son.

"I'm good."

"You sure?" he asked.

"Yep," I said, folding my hands in my lap.

"Alrighty then."

We'd driven about a hundred feet when I blurted, "Are you really not going to fight this?"

"Fuck me," he breathed out.

"You have to fight," I said. "If you don't, you'll be killing your son. And if you hurt that man, I will maim you."

His mouth creeped up into a smile. "Maim me?"

"Maim you," I confirmed. "And from a daughter's perspective, if you don't tell Violet what's going on, you're going to scar her to the bone. So, I ask you, big man, do you want your daughter on a pole, sporting a brand-new septum ring, and 'Daddy' tattooed across her ass?"

Sundance pulled the truck to the side of the road before he lost total control over his laughter. "Jesus Christ," he said once he'd stopped laughing. "I can see why my boy loves you."

I forced the gooey, warm feeling that statement gave me deep into the pit of my stomach. "He loves you more."

Sundance's eyes softened and he sighed. "I highly doubt that, sweetheart, which gives me nothing but happiness."

I stared at my hands and blinked back tears. "Please fight," I whispered.

His big hand covered both of mine and squeezed. "Is he freaked?"

I met his eyes. "Night terror level."

"Jesus," he whispered.

"I know things are… tense between the two of you, but you have to know how much he loves and respects you. You're still his dad. He needs you."

Sundance studied me the way only a father could. "I fucked up."

I bit my lip. "If by that you mean you haven't been *showing* Orion how much you love him? Maybe just a little, because you forgot words don't matter to him. You have to back that shit up with actions."

"You figured that out already, huh?"

"I didn't need to figure it out. It's written in the pages of his whole being."

"Yeah," he breathed out.

"So, you have to fight."

"Yeah."

I smiled, my heart suddenly lighter. "I'll make you soup."

"Soup?"

"When you're dealing with the worst part of chemo. You'll probably be wrecked, and I make a damned good chicken noodle soup, chock full of stuff that will give you strength."

His eyes got soft again and he gave my hands another squeeze. "I can't wait," he said, and pulled back onto the road.

"Since Orion's on a run, would you mind dropping me home?" I asked.

"You're welcome at the cabin, sweetheart."

"Thanks. But I have a few things I need to do, so home would be best."

"Sure thing."

I directed him to my townhouse and he insisted on walking me to my door and waiting for me to step inside.

"Lock up."

"I will," I promised and closed the door, locking it and heading upstairs to cry my eyes out for a few minutes. Or hours. I wasn't sure how long my crying jag would last, just that my heart was breaking for Orion and his dad and I needed to get a grip before I saw Orion again.

* * *

My body being jostled awake was my first indication I'd actually fallen asleep, and then strong arms wrapped around me from behind, pulling me against a hard body. "You weren't at the club when I got there," Orion accused.

"Sorry," I whispered on a yawn, rolling to face him. "I had a few things to get done, so I figured with you being gone anyway, I'd take advantage."

"And did you get everything done?"

"No," I admitted, wrapping an arm around his waist. "Apparently, I fell asleep."

"Anything you want to tell me?"

"Not really."

He kissed me gently and stroked my cheek. "I'm taking Dad to chemo tomorrow."

I searched his face for irritation but found nothing but love. "How do you feel about that?"

"In awe that you're mine, honestly."

I smiled. "So, you don't feel I overstepped my bounds and ignored your edict to be the subservient little woman who doesn't speak until she's spoken to?"

He chuckled. "I see the story gets more elaborate every time you tell it."

"I'm pretty sure I just quoted you warmly and accurately."

"I love you, even if you're crazy."

"Love you back, DC."

He grinned. "You wanna share what you and Dad talked about?"

"I just asked him to fight."

"Jesus. Seriously?" he hissed.

I nodded. "Yes."

He leaned in to kiss me gently. "I don't deserve you."

I grinned. "You better never forget that, buddy."

"Don't ever plan on doing that." He slid off the bed. "You hungry?"

"Yes." I rubbed my eyes. "If you're cooking. I need to study."

"Need help with that?"

"It's microbiology, so, yes, absolutely. Can you multi-task?"

"Not well." He grinned. "But I'll cook, then we'll study."

"Sounds perfect," I said, and followed him downstairs.

For the next two hours, we cooked, we flirted, and Orion tried to explain microbiology to me. Unsuccessfully.

I let out a frustrated groan. "I'm a lost cause."

"Baby, you're not," he said, wrapping an arm around my waist.

I dropped my head to his chest. "Everything you're saying sounds so incredibly smart and I don't understand any of it."

He gave me a squeeze. "I have an idea."

"I don't know if I can handle any more ideas."

He chuckled. "Tomorrow, I'm going to take you on a field trip."

"Where?"

He lifted my chin and smiled. "Can't tell you. But I'll show you tomorrow."

"Fine," I breathed out. "But since we now have the night off, I'd like to eat ice cream off your dick."

"Jesus, woman, you're insatiable."

I raised an eyebrow. "Are you complaining?"

"Not even a little bit." He slid his hands under my T-shirt and stroked my back. "What flavor do you want?"

I grinned. "Rocky Road."

"Let's go."

I grabbed the ice cream and followed him upstairs.

* * *

The next afternoon, I walked out of class to find Orion waiting by his bike. Lordy, the man looked edible in his dark jeans, motorcycle boots, and leather jacket.

"Hi," I said, leaning up on my tiptoes to kiss him. "What are you doing here? I thought you had your dad's chemo appointment."

"All done. He's home and resting comfortably. Letti's on Dad watch," he said.

I frowned. "Okay."

"Did you forget I was taking you on a field trip?"

I smiled. "No, but I thought I was meeting you at the cabin. Much later. Like, way after you took your dad to his appointment."

"Figured we'd go for a little ride."

"My car—"

"Is back at the cabin," he interrupted.

"What?"

"Sierra loaned me your spare key. I had Aero move it, then take the key back to Sierra."

"Seriously?"

He kissed me again. "Yep. Sierra gave Aero your leather jacket and I've got an extra helmet. Come on, we'll throw your shit in the saddlebags."

"Well, you seem to have thought of everything."

He chuckled. "Boy Scouts."

"You were a Boy Scout?"

"Hell, yeah, I was," he said, taking my books from me and handing me my jacket and helmet. "Eagle Scout, baby."

I chuckled. "Well, color me impressed."

He grinned and threw his leg over his bike, waiting for me to climb on behind him. I tightened the strap on my helmet, then slid on and wrapped my arms tight around his waist. We took off and I snuggled close to him, letting the vibration of the bike soothe me.

God, I loved being on the back of a bike, and there was something even more special about being on the back of my man's bike. I was sorely disappointed when we pulled through a ten-foot barbed wire fence and drove up to a huge warehouse at the edge of Colorado Springs.

We climbed off the bike and I removed my helmet and jacket, handing them to Orion after he'd fished my purse out of one of the saddlebags.

He grinned, taking my hand. "This is one of our grow centers."

"Oh, seriously?"

"Yep. Welcome to the house of Frankenflower."

"Frankenflower?"

"Our growers are constantly perfecting new hybrid strains and I can never keep up with all of the names, so I just call them our Frankenflowers."

I chuckled. "Does that make you Dr. Frankenstone?"

He dropped his head back and laughed. "Oh, that's good. I guess that would make Chan Igor."

"Who's that?"

"Paul Chandler. Our lead horticulturist. Come on. I think you need a visual demonstration on how all of this works."

He led me into the building and we were met with all

manner of fancy security. He used a key card to get through the front door, then had to use the card again to get through the foyer doors. "Everything in here is bullet proof," he explained.

"Smart," I said.

Once through the foyer doors, we walked into a large room where two security guards stood by another set of doors.

"Hey, Orion," the older of the two said.

"Hey, Mike." He nodded to the other guard. "Larry. I'd like you both to meet Raquel."

"Hi," I said.

"Nice to meet you," they said.

"Is Chan around?"

"Yeah," Mike said. "He's in the lab."

"Cool," Orion said, and used his keycard again to move through the building.

I gripped Orion's hand as he led me through hallways, past windowed rooms full of plants, and then into a large bright room containing one man, his curly hair a little long and messy, which made him look a bit like a mad scientist. However, instead of wearing a white coat, he wore a rubber apron.

"Hey, Ori," he said, setting the notebook down he'd been writing in.

"Hey. This is Raquel," he said, tugging me forward.

"Nice to meet you," I said, shaking his hand.

"Raquel is having a difficult time in microbiology, so I figured I'd give her a hands-on visual tutoring session."

"My pleasure. Anything I can help with?" Chandler asked.

"How are you with Bacterial Pathogenesis?"

"I develop new and better strains of weed for a living, so that should be an indicator," he replied.

"Don't let Dr. Chandler fool you," Orion said. "The

man is a certifiable genius and can pop and lock better than any white boy should be allowed."

"He's right about that," Chandler said.

"Raquel is researching cannabis for use in treating the symptoms of epilepsy," Orion said.

"That's fantastic," Chandler said. "If you ever need a partner to bounce anything off, my lab door is always open. The world of cannabis can be a confusing place for us geeks."

"Tell me about it," I breathed out.

"I get it." Chandler nodded. "But understanding the hemp plant is easier than you think. You're in good hands around here."

"That's what he tells me," I retorted.

He chuckled. "I'm sure he does."

"If you're done flirting with my girl, I'm gonna show her the grow lab."

"Have fun," he said, and Orion guided me down the hall again and into an entirely different room.

The walls were covered with plants, all labeled, with clipboards hanging below each plant and I leaned forward to read one. Of course, it was Greek to me, but it looked like the details of the plant's origins, along with THC and CBD levels.

There was a bunch of other notes and information, but I had no idea what any of it meant, so I straightened and made my way to the huge table in the middle of the room.

"Whatta ya think?" Orion asked.

"The smell is a bit much," I admitted.

"You get used to it," he said with a smile. "Has the smell or the smoke ever bothered you when you've smoked it?"

I laughed. "I've never smoked weed," I said in a tone that made me sound like a child theater actor in an anti-drug skit.

"Edibles? Vape?" Orion asked, confused.

"I've never gotten high."

Orion paused for a moment, before turning and walking away without a word.

Raquel

T HIRTY SECONDS LATER, Orion reappeared
with a small plastic bag filled with what looked
like green candies of some sort.

"Here," Orion said, placing a small green gummy in
my hand.

"A frog?" I asked with a nervous giggle.

"It's an edible."

"I figured that out. I'm not *that* square," I said.

"The fact you just used the term 'square' sorta says
otherwise, doesn't it?"

"Brat." I smacked Orion's rock-hard chest. "Why do I have it?"

"Because you're going to eat it," he said plainly.

"Why would I do that? I just told you I don't get high. I've never ingested cannabis in any form."

"Well, you'd better buckle up, buttercup, because you're about to," Orion said with a grin.

"My research is purely scientific and aimed entirely at the medical field. I have no interest in the recreational weed market," I said, attempting to give the gummy back to Orion.

"This *is* medical research," he said, refusing.

"How will me getting baked help fight disease?"

"Baked? It's a ten-mil edible, not a trip out to the Mystery Machine with Scooby and Shaggy," he said in an easy laugh that made my heart flutter.

"What if I scromit?"

"Scromit?"

"When you ingest copious amounts of Marijuana, you can scream and vomit uncontrollably."

"That's not a thing."

"Scromiting is absolutely a thing. It's becoming quite prominent in medical journals, as a matter of fact."

Once Orion stopped guffawing enough to breathe, he shook his head and said, "I promise I'll never let you ingest enough pot to scromit, Frazzle."

Orion possessed a natural warmth like no man I'd ever known. Except for maybe his father. And even though I was in a pot lab with a biker who was attempting to give me drugs, I felt as 'safe as kittens' as Nana used to say. I laughed on the inside at the irony of the situation, as this was the exact type of scenario my brother had tried to shield me from my entire life. Not only tried but succeeded. Tristan had always done a great job of protecting me from the dangerous side of his club, while doing his best to promote the best traits of its members.

Of course, the Dogs were a vastly different club from the Howlers in just about every imaginable way, but still. I'd always had a feeling about Orion that made me trust him in a way that I trusted my brother.

"Look, Chan has asthma. Real bad, actually, so he's an expert in all things edible, because he can't smoke. His formulas are world-renowned, but this needs to be your decision, Razzle, and I can give you three reasons why I think you should become friends with Mr. Hoppy there," Orion said, pointing to the edible still clutched within my sweaty hand.

"Oh, really?"

"Really."

"Do tell," I challenged.

"First of all, I meant it when I said I believed it will provide valuable data for your research."

The temperature between my thighs shot up by at least ten degrees. Apparently, I liked it when Orion spoke clinically, just as much as he did when I talked like a biker. I did my best to remain focused on my rebuttal and I licked my lips as I took a deep breath. "I told you, the scope of my research doesn't contain the psychotropic effects of cannabis."

"Maybe you should broaden your scope," he countered. "The whole reason you're studying cannabis in the first place is to fight disease, right?"

"Of course," I replied.

"How do you know the scope of the diseases you can treat with cannabis if you don't know the full effects of the plant itself? Both THC and CBD have their medical benefits, and many effective psychiatric medications produce psychotropic effects."

I opened my mouth to argue, but nothing but puritanical hot air came out, so Orion continued, "Secondly.

You're going to come across a shit ton of people during your research and every one of them is going to have a strong opinion on the subject of pot."

"So?" I asked, which was at least an upgrade from nothing.

"*So*...most of these opinions are gonna be based on third-hand misinformation, anecdotes, fantasy, and utter bullshit. On *both* sides."

"What do you mean?"

"Some people think cannabis is the devil's lettuce, right? It's an evil drug that leads to all kinds of untold debauchery," Orion said in a mock Southern Baptist preacher voice. "Of course, they're wrong, but not without their valid points from time to time. On the other hand, you have pot evangelists that want the world to believe that bong rips cure everything from athlete's foot to brain cancer. Those folks usually just end up muddying the waters of public discussion for medical use."

"So, how does me getting high fix the fact that both sides are wrong?"

"It won't," Orion said.

"Are you sure I'm not stoned already, because I'm really confused. I thought you wanted me to eat the frog?"

Orion laughed softy, gently opened my clenched fist, and took the now warm and gooey edible from me, and held it up.

"I want you to take cannabis so you can relate to both sides. You're a level-headed woman of science, studying within a field charged with high emotions and opinions, and I think it would be cool if you studied every aspect of what people find useful about this little green plant."

Orion had nothing but valid points from a research standpoint, I was doing nothing illegal or unethical, and apart from the high sugar content of the gummy, wasn't putting anything harmful into my body. I was also a grown-ass woman, who was curious, in the company of someone she trusted, and I just so happened to love gummies. I closed my eyes and stuck out my tongue like a parishioner receiving communion. Playing the role of priest, Orion placed the edible on my tongue, which I then chewed and swallowed before opening my eyes.

"You said there were three reasons I should eat the frog, but you only gave me two."

"The third reason's a tad less scientific," Orion said with a grin. "You need a little vacation for a few hours, and I know you well enough to know you're not gonna do that without a little assistance."

"I do not have a problem relaxing," I argued. "I relax whenever I'm not working, studying, or in the lab."

"Which is when exactly?"

"Lately, a lot! In fact, you're a bad influence on my work ethic."

"Me? How do you figure?"

I waved my hands in the air violently. "Look what we're doing right now? I should be at home studying and you just gave me an edible, while using big boy words that are making me horny."

Orion laughed heartily. "We're standing in a lab after school, when you should be relaxing, and the only way you were able to convince yourself to take that edible was to focus on the research benefits."

Once again, Orion saw right through me and spoke his thoughts bluntly, yet kindly.

"Yeah, well. I don't even feel anything, so this was probably all for nothing anyway," I said.

"Edibles aren't like taking a shot of tequila, or even smoking flower, where you begin to feel the effects right away," Orion said.

"How long does it take and when will I know?"

"Usually around an hour, sometimes more, sometimes

less. And don't worry you'll know.

I nodded and Orion kissed me before leading me back into the lab.

* * *

"I swear to god, I'll cut your balls off with the knife in my boot if you lay another skip down, Chan."

Doctor Chandler remained expressionless as he laid his card down.

"I hope you go another year without getting laid," Orion said, staring down at the yellow card, signifying the loss of yet another turn.

"Don't hate the playa," Doctor Chandler deadpanned.

Orion turned to me. "Make him pay, Razzle. Avenge me!" he howled before taking another bong hit.

I checked my phone for the time. "It's been over an hour and I still don't feel anything. Maybe I should eat another frog," I said and started to stand.

"No!" Both Orion and Doctor Chandler shouted.

"It's a bad idea to take more edibles before the first batch kicks in," Orion said, gently sitting me back down. "That's when things can get a little nutty."

"Nutty? What does nutty mean?" I said, starting to panic. "Are things going to get nutty for me?"

"Don't worry, babe. You'll be fine," he said, but his words didn't necessarily make me feel better. In fact, I was starting to feel a little warm. "It's your turn," Orion said, pointing to my cards.

"It's not fair," I said. "You guys are already high, which probably makes UNO more tolerable, but I'm still sober as a judge and will probably turn out to be one of those people who have that liver enzyme that makes edibles ineffective for me. I read a paper on the subject about six months ago. Is it hot in here? I can't remember the name of the enzyme, but it was fascinating. That's a hard word to say. *Fascinating.* It's weird because there's a C in fascinating but you don't say the C when you say fascinating, you just say the word. Which is weird, because I guess that's how all words work. We just saaaaay them, but we never really think about it, do we? That's strange, isn't it? I mean, all the hundreds and thousands of little things we say and do every day that we don't even think about, like saying words. Saying words. Wait, that's not right. Word saying. What's the word for saying words?"

"Talking," Orion said.

"Talking. Right!" I said excitedly before noticing how Orion and Doctor Chandler were looking at me. "Am I talking a lot?"

Orion smiled and said, "It's still your turn."

I looked down at the array of colorful cards I was holding in my hand and instantly began to weep at their beauty. Never had I held such a vibrant display of pulsating color and light within my hands. Tears began to stream down my face as I stared at their magnificent beauty and I wondered why I couldn't recall UNO being such a beautifully moving game when I'd played it in the past. Perhaps this was an updated version.

My lips began to sweat.

Wait? Do lips sweat? Did I just ask that out loud? Did I just ask that out loud, too?

"Razzle?" I heard Orion ask from the other end of the tunnel we were now in.

I tried to answer but my lips were too heavy to move.

"I think Mr. Hoppy is doing his job, Chan," Orion said.

By my estimation it took approximately seventeen minutes for me to complete the following sentence, "I think I'm starting to feel something."

And feel something I did. Panic.

"I think I'm too high. I think I took too much and my

heart is going to explode. Can you guys hear my heart? It's beating super loud right? Am I talking loud?" I asked, fairly sure those words could very well be my last.

I couldn't tell if the boys were trying not to laugh or if the look on their faces was one of concern. It was probably concern. They probably knew I was about to die of a marijuana overdose, and they didn't have the heart to tell me.

"Raquel, honey," Orion said, sweetly. His words momentarily anchoring me back to reality.

"Hmmmm?" I answered.

"You're gonna be okay, you're just high for the first time and a little paranoid. It'll wear off and you'll be good to go. Let's have some candy."

"Candy?" I answered more excitedly than I'd intended, but I had to admit that eating candy sounded like the greatest proposition anyone had ever put forth to me.

For the next three hours I was on a magic carpet ride of gooey deliciousness. Orion was right. After a short while, and a few mini-counseling sessions with my personal guides, the paranoia subsided, and I felt lighter than I ever had.

Orion and Chan were excellent hosts and took turns playing the roles of DJ and dance partner as the lab became our makeshift nightclub. They played all my favorite jams and I danced until I didn't have an ounce of sweat left in my lips. I ate two candy bars from Chan's private stash. Okay, I ate three, but they were filled with pure magic and I regret nothing. My thoughts were both free and yet, hyper focused. I found myself able to attack thoughts from alternative angles yet holding on to them seemed slippery at times. I could already see the benefits Orion and others had talked about but was far from any conclusive thoughts. Right now, I wasn't even sure what a complete thought was.

Somewhere around hour five, I began to get very sleepy and Orion carried me out to his bike...wait, no, not bike. "Where's your bike?"

"Aero came by and swapped it out for Dad's truck. I knew you'd be too tired to hold on."

"You are correct." I gave his neck a squeeze. "Are you okay to drive?"

"Yeah, baby, I'm sober. I haven't smoked for hours."

"Driving while high is just as bad as driving while intoxicated."

"I know, Frazzle. I'm good. I promise."

He chuckled and drove me home, helping me up to my room and undressing me. After he tucked me in, he kissed me on the forehead, and I drifted off to an amazing night of sleep.

* * *

Blinding light jarred me awake and I rolled to get away from it, bumping into Orion. "Sorry," I whispered.

"I forgot to close that drape. My bad."

"Yes, it *is* your bad," I grumbled, sliding my hand over his belly and kissing his chest. "But now I get to snuggle, so I'll forgive you."

Orion grinned as he slid his arm to my waist and gave me a squeeze. "How do you feel?"

"Wiped out, but in a good way." I settled my chin on my hand and met his eyes. "Do you want to talk about your dad's appointment yesterday?"

"There's nothing much to talk about. He sat in a chair with a needle in his arm, surrounded by a few other patients dealing with the same shit. He pretty much ignored me. He was too busy chatting up the woman sitting next to him."

"She was going through chemo?"

"No, her father was. She and dad got on like a house

on fire. Well, no, she and I actually chatted more than he did, but he couldn't take his eyes off her."

"Oh," I said, hopeful. "You think he'll ask her out?"

Orion chuckled. "No, probably not."

"Why not?"

"Babe, Dad's the president of a 1% MC and she's high-class. I'm not sure she'd give him the time of day."

"I'm high-class and I gave you the time of day."

"Because you came into the pit of the beast of your own free will."

I snorted. "Whatever."

"You slummed it and I knew if I didn't lock you down, I'd never have the chance again."

I frowned. "What?"

"The second you walked in, I claimed you, baby. Don't ever doubt it."

Well, that was seriously sweet. My belly got all squishy and I snuggled closer. "I kind of claimed you too."

He gave me a squeeze. "Yeah, I picked up on that."

"Tell me about this woman."

"She's really pretty, probably mid-thirties, and her name's Wyatt."

"That's a way cool name!"

"I know, right?" he admitted. "She and I chatted a bit, but I mostly just hung out and made sure Dad didn't need anything. Once he was done, I drove him home. Letti took over from there."

I sighed. "So, you're okay?"

"Yeah, baby, I'm okay."

"Will you tell me if you're not?"

"Yes. I will tell you if I'm not." He smiled, rolling me onto my back and kissing my neck. "For now, though, burying my dick deep inside your delicious cunt's all the therapy I need."

"Bury it deep, baby."
He did as he was told.

Raquel

ONE MONTH LATER, I had raised my low C grade to a B-plus in microbiology and I was feeling on top of the world. In fact, this particular science was clicking so well, I was currently at the grow lab on my own, working on a new strain with Chan.

"I have two plants for you to look at," Chan said. "We won't be able to test them for another couple of months, but I think you'll like what we have planned."

"Higher Indica strain?" I asked.

"One is, yes. The other—"

He was cut off by the sound of the fire alarm.

"What the hell?" he snapped, then sighed. "I just got

that damn alarm fixed."

"Or we're about to go up in smoke."

"Miss Brooks, did you just make a weed joke?"

I chuckled, admittedly feeling a little proud of myself.

"We may just make a pothead out of you yet."

"I highly doubt I'll ever be the Cheech to your Chong, but I'd hate to see all this research burn."

"Don't worry," he said, shaking his head. "There's never a fire. Just a faulty wire or some shit. But when it happens, the doors lock, so I need to check it out. I'll be right back."

I pulled my cell phone out and sent a text to Orion just in case I didn't get out of here in time to meet him.

Then I waited.

And waited.

Chan didn't return, so I headed to the door and just as I reached out to open it, I felt heat.

"Shit," I whispered, placing my hands flat against the door. It was hot and I was pretty sure I was fucked. I pulled out my cell phone and called 9-1-1.

* * *

Orion

"There's a fire at the warehouse!" Moses bellowed as he rushed past me in the great room.

"What the fuck?" I growled, chasing him. "Raquel's there with Chan."

"Shit!" Moses snapped. "Let's go."

I made a run for my bike and then pulled ahead of Moses on the road, forcing down my panic as we drove to the warehouse.

The stench of pot smoke filled the air, getting stronger as we got closer. By the time we arrived, the east side of the building was engulfed in flames and the Monument

Fire Department were about to turn on their hoses.

I parked my bike and was off it before I'd even killed the engine. I scanned the crowd of onlookers and emergency workers for Raquel and started to panic immediately when I couldn't locate her.

I saw the fire station lieutenant and rushed him. "There was a young woman in the building. Where is she?"

"We were told this place is empty on Sundays," he replied. "Plus, my guys checked the building when we arrived. They didn't find anyone inside."

"I'm telling you, she's in there, along with another guy," I argued.

"Look, I told you. We did a sweep, and no one called out. If they were in there when the fire started, they must have gotten out."

"Raquel would be standing right here if she'd gotten out," I said, turning my eyes toward the building's west entrance.

"Don't even think about it, cowboy," the lieutenant said, clearly reading the look on my face. Not that it mattered. His words had barely left his lips before I took off running.

"Hey, stop that guy," the lieutenant shouted, but I made it to the door before anyone could catch me.

My eyes and lungs burned as soon as I entered the warehouse. Thick black smoke filled the air, making it nearly impossible to breathe or see. I tried to call out but immediately started to choke. My fear rose to terror level as I scrambled to figure out how I was going to find Raquel and Chan, let alone get them out of here before we all choked to death. Then I remembered the supply of portable oxygen tanks we always kept with our first-aid supplies. High altitude can fuck with even the toughest biker, so we always made sure to have a healthy supply of O^2 on hand here and at the clubhouse.

I reached inside my front pocket for the mini mag lite I kept on my keyring, but realized I'd left my keys in the ignition of my still-running bike. I used the flashlight on my cellphone instead, held my breath, and stayed as low as possible as I made my way to the first aid station. I opened the cabinet door and grabbed three portable oxygen cannisters and immediately took a hit off one of them just before passing out. A steady series of bangs caused me to freeze in place. It was difficult to hear over the sound of flames and water kicking the shit out of each other on top of the roof, but after a few seconds, I heard it again. *Whack, whack, whack.*

It was Raquel and I knew exactly where she was. "Goddamn, I love that woman."

I made my way toward the sound, careful to stay low and check the doors as I went. Although the flames seemed to be dying down, the temperature and smoke levels were rapidly rising. However, as I got closer to my destination, the banging stopped, causing my heart to stop as well. What if I was too late?

* * *

Raquel

The building filled with smoke so quickly I barely had time to formulate a plan. The lab's only exit was blocked by flames, made evident by the nasty burns on my hands, courtesy of a hot metal door and an even hotter doorknob. I'd leaned against the door and tried to turn the knob, my hands instantly burning at the effort.

Chan had rushed back to me, the exit to the building also blocked, and an asthma attack took him down almost immediately. His inhaler was in his car and the only place I could think to take him was into the vault. I remembered Orion and Chan talking about its construction and ventilation system and thought we could buy some time before the firefighters found us. I pulled my shirt off and ran it under the lab sink, creating a makeshift mask for us to share and got us into the vault just before Chan collapsed.

The vault's independent ventilation system had clearly been compromised and smoke began to fill up the small space. The temperature of the room was also getting noticeably hotter by the second. I figured at this rate we'd have two, maybe three minutes tops before we either suffocated or roasted to death. Chan was barely conscious as it was, the smoke triggering a massive asthma attack. He was currently lying on the floor, trying to figure out which shade of blue to turn next as he watched me repeatedly bang a metal folding chair, using my wrists to hold it because my hands hurt like motherfuckers, dressed in only my jeans and a bra.

"Don't...worry...," I huffed in between whacks at the door. "Someone will...hear the banging."

Chan gave me a thumbs-up, mustered what I was now sure would be his last smile, and rasped, "Nice view to die to."

Normally I'd be embarrassed, but given the fact that Chan was about to die right in front of me, I was kind of happy the girls could bring him a moment of joy before he died.

"No one is...dying here...today," I said, trying to muster enough strength to bang the chair again, but the truth was, I had no idea if anyone would even be able to hear us from inside this place, and the smoke was now pouring in.

"Save...your...breath," Chan wheezed.

I tried to raise the chair again but failed to lift it above my knees. In my attempt to keep me and Chan safe, all I'd done was find a nice quiet place for us to die. I slumped to the floor completely exhausted as thick black smoke filled the space.

"I'm sorry," I said grabbing Chan's hand and squeezing it tight, but he was out cold, maybe even dead.

I tried to wrap my mind around the fact that these would be my final moments on earth. That, after all these years of wondering, I finally knew how and where I would meet my end. I had to admit, smoke inhalation in a pot lab was never on the list of possibilities of my demise, nor was I particularly crazy about the idea, but it was clearly curtains for me. I managed one final breath and lost consciousness.

I felt myself rise into the air and float through the building. The smell of smoke still present, but more importantly I could smell Orion, and I knew for certain right then I was dead. I was dead and my soul was being carried off to heaven by a biker angel. God made him smell like Orion to comfort me in my time of dying.

"Get the fuck out of my way!" I heard my angel yell.

God even made my angel sound like Orion. But why was he swearing at the other angels?

"You dumb sonofabitch!" I heard another angel yell and began to wonder why there was so much cursing and yelling in heaven.

"I told you they were in there," I heard Orion say and realized I was not dead but being placed on an EMT gurney. My eyes opened and were blinded by flashing red and blue lights. I coughed, causing me to aspirate soot covered mucus. I struggled to breathe and wildly clutched as Orion's arm.

"It's okay, baby. I'm here, I've got you," he said, taking my hand.

"Ch…" was all I managed to get out before violently coughing and hacking.

"Chan's okay. The medics have him now. You're both gonna be okay."

That was the last thing I remember for the next eight

hours.

Raquel

MY FACE ITCHED and my lungs burned. I tried to rub my nose, but my bandaged hand connected with something and I groaned in frustration.

"Oh, my god, Raquel!" Sierra cried, leaning over me. "You're awake."

"Hi," I said, wondering where the hell I was.

"Baby, you gotta keep that oxygen mask on," Orion ordered. "It's helping you breathe."

"Why do I need help breathing?" I mumbled, once again trying to remove the mask, but then it all came rushing back. "The fire." I gasped, then coughed out, "Is Chan okay?"

"Yeah, baby, we got him out."

"What about the plants?"

"The sprinklers did their job. Kind of. The area where you were malfunctioned, so the sprinklers failed. We lost some plants, but none of that really matters, though, because you and Chan were the priority."

I pushed on the mask again. "I get it. But I'm still glad things are salvageable."

"I swear to God, Razzle, you keep messing with that mask, I'm gonna cuff you to the bed."

I couldn't stop a smile. "Kinky."

"Put that back on," he demanded, settling it on my face again.

"But you smell like a campfire. It's nice."

"You two need to get a room," Sierra retorted. "Oh, wait, you're in one. I'd ask if I could hang out and watch, but I have to work. I'm going to come back right after, though, so don't be naked."

I wrinkled my nose. "Technically, I'm already naked. Hospital gowns can't be considered actual clothing."

"Well, keep that on," Sierra ordered. "I called your brother, so you're welcome."

She rushed out of the room before I could verbally spank her. Great. Tristan. That would mean my parents, and, well, crap. How was I going to explain being caught in a fire in a grow house?

"It's going to be okay," Orion said, interrupting my thoughts.

"My dad's going to lose his mind."

"I already talked to your brother. He's coming, but he's playing interference with your parents and little brothers. He wants to assess the situation, then go from there."

I relaxed a little. "Oh, thank god."

123

He smiled and squeezed my hand. "You freaked me out."

I shrugged. "I knew you'd save me."

"Bullshit."

"I did," I argued.

He lifted my fingers to his lips. "Smart getting your T-shirt wet, baby. I'm glad you had the wherewithal to do that. Not so glad you were only in your bra when I found you, though. Jesus, Chan was probably hard while he was passing out."

I rolled my eyes. I'd pulled my T-shirt off and wet it, then wrapped it around my nose and mouth, getting as low as I could as the smoke grew worse. Doom, the VP of my brother's club, had been a fireman for years before he moved on to other vocations. He still had a lot of stories, and told them often, and talked about how important it was to block the smoke and get low.

"I knew you'd find me," I said.

"What if it hadn't been me?"

"So?"

"So?" he hissed. "Your tits are the kind that'll bring a man to his knees, Razzle. But they're mine and I don't want any other asshole enjoying the view. I'm already contemplating beating the shit out of Chan the second he wakes up."

I pulled the mask off, finding it difficult to argue with him with it on. "You are insane."

"Put that back on," he ordered, placing the mask back on my face.

"Quit bugging me, Smoky," I admonished.

"Smoky?"

"Your new name."

He shook his head. "Are you the Bandit?"

"Abso-fucking-lutely."

He sighed. "Baby, don't be so flippant."

"Don't worry. I'm okay," I said.

"Maybe. But until the doctor clears you, I'm gonna worry."

I nodded, a coughing fit suddenly overtaking me.

"Jesus," Orion hissed and rushed into the hallway. "I need a doctor!"

For the next two hours, I was poked and prodded, forced to take in copious amounts of oxygen and generally made to feel miserable. Well, I suppose the burns on my hands from stupidly trying to open the door by touching the hot handle were making me miserable, but regardless, I wanted everyone out so I could sleep.

"Orion?" I whispered.

"Yeah, baby."

"Find me some morphine, then make them go away."

Within minutes, my man had cleared the room, pressed the button on my pain pump (that I had no idea I was hooked up to), and turned out the lights.

"Sleep, Frazzle. I'm right here."

I closed my eyes and let the morphine take me away.

* * *

Orion

As soon as I knew Raquel was asleep, I stepped out of her room and pulled out my phone, calling Moses.

"Hey, brother," he said after answering on the first ring.

"You better have a fuckin' update for me."

"I told you I'd call you when I got any."

I scowled. "Yeah, but my woman's in a hospital bed because those assholes fucked with our club. I want them fuckin' dealt with, but Jaws is mine."

"You want the prez, brother, we're gonna have to do this smart," Moses said.

"Yeah, I hear you," I growled. "But I'm reiterating the fact that no one but me deals with him."

"Got it," he said and sighed. "How's Raquel?"

"Asleep. But she was in a lotta pain before that."

"Burns on your hands are a motherfucker," Moses said, and he should know...he was a firefighter in Savannah for years before moving to Colorado. "She's gonna need help to do basic things for a while."

My anger swamped me again. "Yeah."

"You need anything, you let me know."

"I need Jaws in the basement so I can have a conversation with him."

"Okay, brother. We're workin' on that. I'm gonna let you go."

"Okay," I said, and hung up, stepping back into Raquel's room.

She looked so small in the huge hospital bed and it broke my heart knowing she was in pain. Jesus, the Predators' were gonna fuckin' pay.

"Where did you go?" Raquel whispered as I sat in the chair next to her.

"Nowhere, baby."

"Will you get me a nurse, please?"

I stood and leaned over her. "Why? Are you in pain?"

"No, honey. I need to pee."

I nodded. "Be right back."

I grabbed a nurse, then waited outside the room while Raquel got comfortable.

"She's good now," the nurse said, holding the door open for me, and I headed back inside the room.

"Will you sleep with me?" Raquel asked.

"Sure." I climbed on the bed and pulled her gently toward me. "Watch your hands."

"I'm okay," she rasped, dropping her head to my chest. "I just need to feel safe right now. Hands be damned."

"I'm sorry, baby," I whispered, stroking her back.

"I'm good now. I just need you to stay here, okay?"

"Not goin' anywhere, Razzle. I promise."

She nodded into my chest and I held her until she fell asleep. I slid my phone out of my pocket and set the alarm, making sure to hit her pain pump before I let myself sleep as well.

Four hours later, my alarm beeped, and I silenced it as quickly as I could, trying not to wake Raquel. I hit her pain pump, then set my alarm for another four hours before falling back to sleep. I wasn't asleep for long when my phone beeped again, but this time, it wasn't my alarm.

It was Wrath.

"Hey," I whispered into the phone.

"It wasn't Jaws," Wrath said.

"Bullshit."

"We've got proof."

"Who was it?"

"Zilla."

"Jesus fucking Christ," I hissed, and Raquel stirred beside me. "Sorry, baby, go back to sleep." I slid off the bed and stepped into the hallway. "What the fuck crawled up that dinosaur's ass?"

Zilla was actually only twenty, and he was a newly patched member for the Predators.

"Figured you could ask him," Wrath said. "He's here."

Now that the fire breathing little prick had earned his patch, my guess was he was trying to make his bones. If that was the case, this bastard was gonna lose his arms. He couldn't ride without arms, which would mean he couldn't patch into an MC. No bike, no life. "Okay. Gotta make sure Raquel's okay first. Don't let him out of your sight."

"No problem. I'm having a little fun with him."

"Just keep him lucid," I ordered.

"Killjoy."

"See you in a bit."

"Okay, brother."

Wrath hung up and I slid my phone into my pocket. I walked back into Raquel's room to find her trying to get out of bed.

"Baby, what the hell are you doing?"

"I have to pee."

"Let me help you."

"No way in hell," she ground out. "We are not at the 'wipe my puss' level of our relationship."

I chuckled. "I can lick it, but not wipe it?"

"Oh, my god." She groaned. "Yes. Exactly."

"Stay here," I ordered, laying my hands on her shoulders. "I'll get a nurse."

"You can just press the call button, Smoky."

"Right," I said, and fished the wire out of the mattress, pressing the red button.

A nurse arrived a few minutes later and helped Raquel with her personal stuff while I waited in the hallway.

"What the fuck is going on?"

I turned to the sound of my father's angry voice.

"What are you doing here?" I asked. "You're supposed to stay isolated during chemo."

"Why the hell was Raquel at the warehouse, Ori?" Dad demanded, crossing his arms.

"She's doing research for her thesis."

He shook his head and I saw just how wiped out he was.

"Dad, sit dow—"

"Don't tell me to fuckin' sit down."

"Raquel has asked that you both come inside," the nurse said, interrupting us.

I led my dad inside, and Raquel frowned. "Why are you here, Sundance? You should be resting."

He walked to her and leaned down, kissing her cheek.

"How are you feelin'?"

"I'm okay. How are you feeling?"

"Don't worry about me, kiddo."

She sighed. "You shouldn't be in a germy hospital with a weakened immune system, crazy man."

"Well, if my kid kept me updated on shit, then maybe I wouldn't have to."

"You don't need to be updated on shit," I snapped. "You need to be dealing with your health."

"Sundance, would you please sit down before you fall down?" Raquel asked.

I pulled a chair close to my dad and waited for him to lower himself into it.

"Okay, now that I'm sitting... Why the fuck was she at the warehouse, Orion?" Dad growled.

"Because I'm working on my thesis," Raquel answered.

"She should never have been there alone," Sundance continued.

"Hey!" Raquel snapped. "I'm here in the room with you, big man. I'm quite capable of answering your questions all by myself."

"I don't want answers from you, Raquel. I want to know why my son left you in a grow house alone."

"He didn't leave me alone. I had two armed security officers and Chan there with me. Also, Ori only left for half an hour to grab something I'd forgotten to bring with me, so would you please give him a break?"

"What if Raquel hadn't made it out of there?" Dad continued, totally ignoring Raquel's request.

"That wasn't an option," I said.

"It's always an option!" Dad growled. "You weren't fuckin' there!"

"Yeah! I know!" I ground out.

"I don't think you do, goddammit. If you did, you

would have been there!"

"Like you were with Mom?" I sneered, suddenly realizing I was pissed at him. More than I'd ever been pissed at anyone, which confused me because I was sure I'd dealt with all this shit.

Raquel let out a quiet gasp. "Okay, wait. Let's not let this conversation—"

"Yeah, exactly like your mom," Sundance snapped. "You have to be more vigilant, son."

"You mean, do what you say, not what you do?"

"Orion!" Raquel admonished.

"Yeah, that's exactly what I mean," Dad said.

"Well, you don't have to worry, Dad, I'm a hell of a lot more vigilant than you—"

"Stop!" Raquel snapped, tears streaming down her face. "Both of you, please stop."

Dad pushed up from the chair and nodded. "I'm gonna go ahead and leave now."

He stepped over to Raquel, leaned down and kissed her cheek. "Sorry, baby girl," he said, then walked out the door. I sat in the chair he'd vacated, but my woman was having none of it.

She threw her arm out, pointing to the door. "You follow him!"

"Razz—"

"You get your ass out the door and follow him."

"Babe—"

"And you apologize. Get down on your knees and beg if you have to."

"Are you serious?" I asked.

"As a fucking heart attack," she hissed. "Your dad is sick. You might not have him for long, so you need to make this right. We'll figure out your other emotions later."

"Other emotions?"

"The ones you obviously haven't completely dealt with." She pointed to the door again. "Move."

Feeling like an errant child, I made my way out of the room and found my dad talking with Raquel's brother and Rabbit.

What the fuck was Rabbit doing here?

"Hey," I said, eyeing up my competition.

Rabbit gave me a shit eating grin and I forced down irritation.

Doc gave me a chin lift. "She awake?"

"Ah, yeah, she's definitely awake."

He nodded and led Rabbit into Raquel's room, leaving me standing with Dad in the hallway.

"You gonna get down on your knees now?" Dad asked.

"You heard that, huh?"

"Pretty sure the whole floor heard it."

"Right. I'm sorry our conversation went to a place it didn't need to go."

"We obviously have a few things to work out," Dad said.

"I'd like to put a pin in that until we sort this shit out with the Predators and your cancer."

He sighed. "I can get behind that."

"Give me a few and I'll drop you home."

"I don't ride bitch, Ori. But it doesn't matter. I drove."

"You fuckin' drove?" I snapped. "Jesus, Dad, have you lost your fuckin' mind?"

"I'm fine."

"Bike or truck?"

"Truck."

"Give me a few minutes. I'm still gonna drop you home."

He sighed. "I don't need you to—"

"Not up for discussion," I hissed, holding my hand out.

"Keys."

He slammed his keys into my palm and lowered himself into one of the benches against the wall.

"I'll be right back," I said, and headed back to Raquel's room.

* * *

Raquel

"Jesus Christ, what the fuck did you do to yourself?" Tristan asked, walking into my room.

"You're here!"

"Yeah, sissy, of course I'm here."

I reached my arms out and he immediately wrapped me in a hug, which gave me a view of Rabbit. "You too?"

"Yeah, sweetheart," Rabbit said, and kissed my cheek. "How ya feelin' there?"

"Better than I probably should," I admitted, and turned to my brother. "Did you tell Mom and Dad?"

He shook his head. "No. But I'm going to as soon as I know the extent of your injuries."

I sighed. "Will you downplay it, please?"

"Let me talk to your doctor and we'll go from there," he said.

I nodded. "Is Liv with you?"

"No. She's home with the twins."

I blinked back tears. "You didn't need to come."

"You seriously think I'd stay away?" he asked.

"Why am I always walking into a room you're in and my woman's crying?" Orion demanded, walking back in.

"I'm fine, Ori," I said. "Did you talk to your dad?"

"Yeah. I need to drop him home and head back to the cabin to take care of a few things. You gonna be here for a while?"

This question was for my brother who said he wasn't

going anywhere.

Orion kissed me gently. "You okay if I leave for a few hours?"

"I'm fine, Smoky."

He rolled his eyes. "If you need me, text me."

I held my hands up. "That's not gonna happen."

He grimaced. "Right. Make your brother text me."

I nodded and he kissed me again.

"Be safe," I said.

"Always," Orion said, then he was gone.

"Let me look at your hands," Tristan said, and I reached one out to him.

"Why are you here?" I asked Rabbit. "Did you get permission from Parker?"

"Raquel," he said, his tone one of warning.

"You need to get on that, honey," I continued. "Actually, you should just get on *her*. I can't believe she's been able to resist you this long."

"Leave him alone, sissy," Tristan warned as he gently pulled out his penlight and unwrapped my bandage, studying my hand. "Does the other look like this?"

"No. It's better than this."

He sighed. "Second degree burns are no joke, sissy, but it looks like it's healing the right way." He wrapped me back and gave me a gentle smile. "Your life's gonna suck for a couple of weeks, though."

"Yeah. I'm aware."

"I'm gonna stay for a few days. Do you want me at your place, or at the cabin?"

"You're staying?" I asked. "Why?"

"To make sure you're okay."

"*And...*" I prompted.

"I'm gonna help the Howlers out with a minor issue they've got."

"This 'minor issue' started the fire, didn't it?" I deduced.

"Not sure."

"Tristan," I said with a frustrated sigh. "I'm not an idiot."

"Fair enough." He smiled.

"So?"

"So?" he parroted.

"What's going on?"

"Still not discussing this with you," he said and smiled. "Are Rabbit and I staying with you or at the club?"

"Either's good with me, but if you're at the club, I will be, too. I don't want to miss out on time."

"And Sierra might try to climb into bed with me if I'm at your place."

"That happened once," I pointed out and Tristan chuckled.

"Twice."

I gasped "What? Seriously?"

"Yeah. Once I explained where I was with Olivia, though, it didn't happen again."

"Thank god for small favors, I guess," I grumbled.

"Yeah, we'll go with that," he said.

"We'll definitely need to keep her away from you, buddy," I said to Rabbit. "Unless, you want a drop-dead gorgeous, overly sexed woman climbing into bed with you."

"I'm good," he said, and I grinned. He obviously had it bad for Parker.

"I'll talk to Sundance and figure it out," Tristan said.

I nodded, fighting back a yawn.

"Why don't you sleep for a bit. We'll hang out here while you rest."

"Okay." I closed my eyes and let my exhaustion win.

Orion

W ALKING INTO THE cabin, I found Wrath and discovered he was done having fun with Zilla.

"Is he lucid?" I asked.

"Well, he wasn't an hour ago, but I'm pretty sure he is now."

"Jesus, Wrath, what happened to being careful?" I asked.

"I *was* careful. He's still breathin'."

I dragged my hands down my face. "I'm gonna take it from here."

"Have at it."

I made my way downstairs and into the panic room, where I found Aero guarding the door to our 'confession' booth. We'd built the basement out to be comfortable should we need a place to hole up during bad weather or enemy attack. We also had some escape routes that were only known by the club, so if we needed to get out without being seen, we could.

We'd built a room within that space as a panic room, should someone penetrate the basement, but it had become useful to 'question' people should we need to do so where their screams wouldn't be heard. We didn't use it often, mostly because things had been somewhat peaceful over the past few years, but if the fucking Predators decided to come at us again, I had a feeling this room was gonna be used often.

"Hey, Ori," Aero said, giving me a chin lift.

"Hey," I said. "How's the asshole?"

"Just checked on him and he pissed, so he's good."

I nodded. "I'm gonna talk to him. Ignore any screaming."

"From you or him?"

I smirked and pushed open the door. Godzilla, whom everyone called Zilla, was zip tied to a chair, and it appeared as though Wrath had used his brass knuckles to improve his face. Zilla raised his head and scowled. "The prodigal son," he spat out.

I ignored his bullshit jab. "You gonna tell me why you tried to kill my woman?"

"No one tried to kill your woman."

"Then tell me why you set my grow house on fire with her in it."

"Bullshit." His eyes widened slightly. "The building was empty."

"See, Zilla, it wasn't empty. This is the problem."

I pulled a zippo from my pocket and walked around

his chair, flicking the lighter lid open, then closed.

Open, then closed.

"She was trapped inside while the fire burned her end of the building…because you disabled the sprinkler system," I said, continuing to open and close the zippo. "So, this leads me to believe you weren't working alone, because I know for a fact you're a dumb piece of shit. So dumb, in fact, your club looks to you for the jobs that require brawn over brains and no one would expect you to disable shit." I faced him and crossed my arms. "Who was with you?"

"No one, it was just me."

I grabbed his hand tied to the chair, flicked the lighter open and lit it, holding the flame under Zilla's palm. He screamed in pain, trying to pull away from me, but he didn't have the leverage.

"Hurts like a mother fucker, huh?" I said, swallowing the bile threatening to spill from the smell of burning flesh. "Kinda like my woman's hands are feeling right now. You see, she burned them trying to escape the fire you set."

"Collateral damage," Zilla sneered.

I flicked the lighter open again and repeated my 'encouragement' on his other hand, wanting him to hurt worse than Raquel hurt.

He screamed again, but still wouldn't give up his accomplice, so I continued to switch back and forth between his hands until he passed out from the pain.

"Fuckin' pussy," I hissed, opening the cabinet on the wall and pulling out ammonia and waving it under his nose as I pressed on his sternum. He came awake with growl of pain, disoriented and ready to fight. "Welcome back," I said. "You ready for more?"

I pulled my knife from my boot and studied it.

"Orca!" he screamed as I flicked open the zippo again.

I cocked my head. That was a surprise and I'd definitely need more intel on him before I acted on that information. Orca was old school. A faithful soldier. He'd been part of the Predators for more than twenty years and usually kept his head down.

"Anything else?"

"Sonja Myers. She's fuckin' Orca. It was all her idea."

That fucking cunt!

"Thanks, buddy," I crooned. "I appreciate that. I'm gonna let you sit here for a while and then we'll decide what to do with you."

"You gonna get me ice for my hands, asshole?" he snapped.

"Did my woman get ice for *her* hands?"

He scowled.

"I'll let you sit here and think about that," I said and walked out the door, closing it on the obscenities he bellowed behind me.

"Did you have fun?" Aero asked.

"Wait two hours, then get Needles to look at him."

"Don't think acupuncture's gonna cure what's ailing him."

Needles was our resident medical specialist. He had a medical degree, but after a few years, he decided he'd focus on acupuncture. He was hippy dippy in a lot of ways, so the new focus suited him.

"If it's something Needles can't handle, Raquel's brother'll be here in a few hours. He can take over."

"Doc's comin'?"

"Yep," I said. "Text me if you need something."

I made my way upstairs and found Wrath in the kitchen.

"You got what you need?" he asked.

"Orca assisted."

"Shit, no kidding?"

I nodded. "I'm gonna head out for a bit, but I'll be back at the hospital in about an hour."

"Okay, brother. We'll keep Zilla alive."

"Thanks."

I made my way to my bike and took off for my dad's place.

Letting myself into my childhood home, I walked back to Dad's den. "Pops?"

"Shhh!" Violet hissed. "He's asleep."

I pivoted and found her standing in the archway that led to the kitchen. "Hey."

"What are you doing here?" she asked, walking away from me. "I thought you'd be at the hospital."

I followed her. "Needed to take care of a few things."

"How's Raquel?"

"On the mend."

She raised an eyebrow. "Shouldn't you be there?"

"Her brother's with her. Needed to talk to Dad."

"Doc's here?" she asked, pulling a bottle of wine from the rack.

"Yeah. He'll be here for a few days, I think."

"And Olivia?"

"No, she's home with the kids. What's with the twenty questions?" I asked, leaning against the kitchen counter. "You okay?"

"No."

I held my arms open and my sister made her way to me and hugged me tight. "He's dying."

"Not yet he's not."

"He's losing his hair."

"That happens with chemo."

She shrugged, taking a deep breath. "But it doesn't happen to our dad."

"Whoa, what the hell? You okay, Letti?" Drake asked walking into the kitchen.

139

"Yes. Now, shush, Dad's finally asleep."

"No, I'm not," Dad grumbled, joining us. "What the fuck's goin' on? Why's Letti cryin'?"

"Because you're fucking dying," she growled.

He laughed, pulling her into his arms. "I'm not dying. Not by a longshot."

She squeezed him tight. "You better not be lying."

"Baby girl, this is the easiest cancer to beat. It's gonna suck for a few months, but I'm not worried," he said. "Don't worry about the hair. It's gonna grow back."

"Okay."

"You cookin'?" Dad asked Drake.

"Yeah, I guess."

"What else do you have to do?"

"Oh, maybe seeing Alyssa."

"Still?" I raised an eyebrow. "Wow, that's like a month."

My brother loved women. A lot. And he tended to go through them like underwear, so the fact this woman had made it more than a week was kind of a miracle.

"Fuck you," Drake retorted.

Dad chuckled. "You start cookin'. I'm gonna talk to Ori for a minute."

"Are you eating?" Drake asked me.

"Yeah, that'd be great, thanks," I said and followed Dad back to his den.

He closed the door and leaned against it. "So, it wasn't Jaws."

I shook my head. "Orca and Zilla."

"Fuck me," he said, flopping onto the sofa against the wall.

I pulled one of his chairs to the edge of the sofa and sat down, stretching my legs out and setting my feet on a sofa cushion. "Zilla and I had a really nice conversation. He's not gonna be able to jerk off for at least a month."

"Do I want to know?"

"Probably not," I admitted.

"How's Raquel?"

"Hurtin'."

"Jesus, we're gonna need to nip this shit in the bud."

"Agreed." I dragged my hands down my face. "Sorry about the shit I said about Mom."

"About that," he said, leaning forward and settling his elbows on his knees.

I watched him closely. My dad was a straight shooter and he tended to tell me more than my siblings, but I could never get a read on what he was thinking by the expressions on his face. He would have made a great poker player, totally unlike Raquel.

"I don't want to fight, Pops," I said.

"Me neither, but there's something you need to know." He met my eyes. "You think you can stay calm?"

"Jesus, what the fuck?"

My dad sat back again. "That's a no."

I sat up and leaned forward, taking a deep breath in an effort to appear calmer than I was. "Tell me."

Dad dropped his head. "Your mom wasn't killed by a drunk driver."

"The cops arrested a guy."

"I know," he said.

"Dad, spit it out. Jesus, you've come this far."

"Your mom's death was a hit. On me."

I stayed as quiet as I could, my heart in my throat, my blood suddenly running cold.

"Her car had a flat that morning, so she took my truck," he rasped.

My throat burned with impending tears, the memories from the day of my mother's death flooding back.

"Who?"

"Kong."

Kong used to be the Apex Predators' president, before he disappeared. Six days after he'd gone missing, his burned remains were found deep in the woods.

I swallowed. "How?"

"They followed her from the cabin, ran her off the road, and shot her."

"They fuckin' shot her?" I hissed.

"Yeah. There was no way in hell I was telling any of you that at the time. It was hard enough you lost your mom, I didn't want that visual in your head."

"But the news would have reported it."

"We paid off a few people to keep it quiet." He sighed. "Not sure how much longer we can keep it buried, though. I have it on good authority the Predators are being investigated, and this may come out."

"Fuck," I whispered. "Who was the drunk guy at the scene?"

"Some homeless guy they picked up the morning of, drugged, then left in the driver seat of the beater car they had at one of their shops."

"Kong?"

My dad looked at me and I knew what he was going to say, but I didn't stop him from making his confession. "I made him hurt before I killed him."

I pressed my palms to my eyes, trying to ward off a headache. "So, the warehouse is payback."

"No. Jaws and I had an agreement. This is something different. I don't think Jaws knew what Zilla and Orca were doin'. And Wrath mentioned Sonja orchestrated this?"

"When did you talk to Wrath?"

"Five minutes after you left Orca."

Of course he did. Dad was always in the loop, almost in real time. It was evidence of how much our brothers respected him.

"Yeah," I confirmed.

"Jesus Christ. Today's the first time in my life I've ever wanted to kill a woman."

"Fuck, seriously. Stupid cunt."

"No doubt," Dad agreed.

"Coup?" I deduced.

"Yeah, that's where I'm leaning."

"God help anyone who gets in the middle," I breathed out.

"Well, unfortunately, we're in the middle."

"Shit," I said. "We are."

"I called Hatch for backup. I was gonna fly out there when he got back from London, but I'm not sure I'll be able to fly."

I nodded. "I'll go if you can't."

"You need to wrap Raquel in bubble wrap." He sat back, suddenly looking deathly tired. "In fact, she should move into the cabin for a while."

"She won't leave Sierra."

"Both of them, then," Dad said.

"What about Letti and Drake?"

"They're safe here. I've got a few guys on the house."

"Who's taking you to and from chemo if I'm not around?"

"Moses. He drops me off, then picks me up when I'm done."

"You don't want him to stay, huh?"

"No way in hell," Dad said.

I raised an eyebrow. "Letti's okay with not being there?"

"Letti doesn't have a fuckin' choice. She's in school and that takes priority."

"I should take you."

He shook his head. "Need you to watch your woman, Ori. If anything happened to her because of this shit and you weren't there, it'd wreck you. Take it from me."

"I got her, Dad," I promised. "What a fuckin' nightmare."

"Yeah," Dad agreed.

Drake banged on the door and yelled, "Grub's up!"

"I got this, Dad," I said. "I'm all in."

"Fuckin' finally!" he retorted. "Let's eat."

I nodded and followed him into the kitchen.

Raquel

THE NEXT DAY, I was released into my brother's care. There was no point in me staying in the hospital when I had someone who could take care of me, and I wanted out.

The problem was, Orion wouldn't let me go home. I was ushered to the cabin without delay, and without any personal items.

"You're not going back to your townhouse, Razzle," Orion decreed. "Make a list of what you need and I'll have Sierra pack it when I go pick her up."

I held my hands up. "I can't make a list, Orion. I can't

hold a pen or a phone."

"You tell me what you want, and I'll write it down."

"Honey, it would help if I could direct traffic, so to speak, so I don't forget anything."

He dragged his hands through his hair. "Raquel, I'm not taking any chances, so, no."

"You can't say no. I need underwear."

"I'll pack your underwear."

"Gah! You're driving me crazy with all this," I snapped. "I'll have my brother take me."

"Like hell you will. Doc's in agreement with me."

"Yeah, well, I know how to get around my brother."

"But you don't know how to get around me."

I held my hands up again. "If I had use of these, there'd be a lot of ways I could get around you."

He smiled…finally. "There is that."

"Please take me with you, Smoky. You'll protect me."

Orion sighed. "If Wrath and your brother can come with us, I'll take you."

I nodded. "Okay. Thanks."

My brother made time for me and instead of Wrath, Rabbit tagged along which didn't make Orion happy, but he knew he'd help keep me safe.

We pulled up to the townhouse and my brother and Orion did a sweep while I waited outside with Rabbit. Once the all-clear was given, I walked inside and led Orion upstairs while Rabbit and Tristan waited for Sierra.

"I've got a duffel and a suitcase in my closet," I said, and Orion grabbed both and set them on the bed.

I spent the next fifteen minutes instructing Orion on what to pack, including a set of sheets from the linen closet because there was no way in hell I was sleeping (more than one night) on the sheets in his room at the cabin.

"Babe, you don't actually need this many pairs of panties."

"Oh, really?" I asked.

"You won't be wearin' them much."

I rolled my eyes. "Dream on, handsome."

He grinned and continued to pack my bags.

"Do I get to share your room?" I heard Sierra ask.

"Probably not," Rabbit responded.

"Come on," she cajoled. "You can be my Velveteen Rabbit and I'll rub you 'til you shed."

"Yeah, I'm not taking any chances of you pulling out my whiskers," Rabbit retorted.

I forced myself not to laugh. Of course Rabbit knew the story of the Velveteen Rabbit. He seriously seemed to know everything.

Orion raised an eyebrow and gave me a smirk.

"She's insatiable," I warned. "She's going to work her way through the club."

Orion chuckled. "She'll have at least a week to do it."

I frowned. "You really think we'll be there for a week?"

"Yeah, baby, 'fraid so."

"What's going on?" I asked.

He glanced behind him, then made his way to my door and closed it. Sitting on the edge of my bed, he pulled me between his legs. "Shit's goin' down with another club. We're expecting retaliation, so I want you where I know you'll be safe."

"And Sierra might be collateral damage," I finished.

"Yeah."

"They set the fire?"

He tugged me closer, kissing my neck. "I'm not going into any more details about this, Razzle. Just trust that we have it under control."

"I'm going to let this lack of information slide because I've already figured out what happened, but forewarning for next time, I probably won't be so patient." I kissed him quickly. *"Capisce?"*

He grinned, giving my butt a squeeze. "You need me to pack anything else?" he asked, and it wasn't lost on me that he didn't acknowledge my forewarning.

I shook my head. "I'm good."

He kissed me again and we headed out.

* * *

The next three days were an exercise in how not to murder another human being.

That human being was Sierra.

And the person wanting to murder her was Orion.

This meant, I was constantly in the middle of my man and my best friend and I was a little over it.

"I swear to Christ," Orion hissed as he walked into his bedroom.

I was folding laundry on the bed, at least, I was trying to fold since it was about the only thing I could manage with my hands still bandaged. "No."

He closed the door and crossed his arms. "She needs a leash."

"I warned you," I pointed out.

"Babe—"

"No," I repeated, facing him. "I get that you two butt heads. You're both alpha to the core, so it doesn't surprise me. Yes, she's a lot sometimes, unapologetically, but there's a reason she's my best friend. You will never find anyone more loyal or kind. It all just happens to be wrapped up in a tiny free-loving package."

"I don't care that she's having a little fun, Raquel. I didn't even care that she instructed two of my prospects to fuckin' pull everything out of the kitchen cabinets and move things around to 'unblock the flow of chi' or 'release the energy' or what the fuck ever."

"Yes, you did," I countered.

148

"Okay, well, in comparison to what she just did, the kitchen cabinets were nothing."

I dropped a t-shirt on the bed and focused on him. "What happened?"

"She had the same dumbass prospects move Gertrude."

"Who's Gertrude?"

"The 1926 Harley Wrath has been restoring for the past two years."

My stomach roiled. "She moved it?"

"Yeah."

"Did she say *why* she moved it?"

"She said it made the room look unkempt." He dragged his hands down his face. "It's a fucking garage, Raquel."

I bit my lip in an effort not to smile. 'Unkempt' was one of Sierra's favorite words. "Just ask her to put it back."

"Raquel, we are so far beyond that, it's not even funny."

"Why?"

"Because Wrath lost his shit and Sierra's sobbing in the bunk room."

"Oh my god, she's *crying*? Way to fucking bury the lead, *Adam*," I growled as I rushed past him and out of the room. I found my best friend in a puddle, curled up in the fetal position on one of the lower bunkbeds. "Sierra?"

"Go away," she grumbled.

I closed the door and made my way to her, sitting on the edge of the mattress. "Honey, are you okay?"

"Does it look like I'm okay?" she snapped. "This place is full of hostile energy."

"Do you think it might have been a bad idea to move the bike?"

"I do now!" she cried out. "I was just trying to help.

149

You know, give the place a little more hominess."

"Honey, it's a biker club. Hominess doesn't really apply."

"Yeah, well that beast of a man made sure I was fully versed in that fact."

I forced a smile. "I'm sure he'll apologize when he calms down."

"He called me a hippy bitch, Raquel," she whispered. "I don't know that an apology will be sufficient."

I sighed. This was unfortunately true. 'Hippy' Sierra could handle, but you didn't call her a bitch and come out unscathed. "I'm sorry."

"I want to go home."

"I know," I said. "I do, too."

"How long do we need to stay here?"

I shook my head. "I have no idea."

"I have to work tonight," she said.

"I'm aware. Orion is sorting out someone to go with you."

"Well, it better not be that asshole, or I'm gonna open a can of whoop-ass on him."

"Since we definitely don't want that, I'll make sure it's not Wrath, okay?"

She nodded.

"Are you hungry?"

She wiped her cheeks and nodded again. "Yeah, a little."

I rose to my feet. "Let's go see what they have in the fridge, huh?"

* * *

Six hours later, I was walking downstairs when I heard yelling, followed by breaking glass, then more yelling. I inched my way around the corner and saw Wrath jabbing a finger toward Orion, rage an inadequate adjective to describe his mood.

"Outside, Orion!" Wrath bellowed. "Scooby and Scrappy put Gerty outside like a fuckin' dog."

"Where are they?" Orion asked, his voice calm, but tight.

"If they're smart, they left town," Moses retorted. "Maybe they split with that pain in the ass granola chick."

"What do you mean, she left?" Wrath asked, and my heart dropped into my stomach.

"Does it matter? The bitch fuckin' left."

"Yeah, it fuckin' matters, Moses," Wrath growled.

Moses shrugged. "If you find her, you might want to get your woman to reel her hippy friend in."

Shit!

I pulled my phone out of my pocket and fired off a text, using speech to text because my hands were useless, asking Sierra where she was. Three dots appeared, then disappeared, then appeared again.

Sierra: I'm taking a time-out.
Me: Where are you taking this time-out?
Sierra: I don't want to tell you.
Me: I need you to tell me, Sierra, or you'll have to deal with Wrath.
Sierra: That asshole can go fuck himself in the ass.
Me: I need to know you're safe.
Sierra: I'm with Leith. He's keeping me safe.

I bet he was.

Jesus.

Leith was her ex and happened to be the biggest douche on the planet. I rubbed my temples and took a deep breath. This was bad.

Really, really bad.

I headed out of my pseudo-hiding place and when Orion saw me, he stalked toward me. "Any idea where your

151

girl is?"

I nodded. "It's not good, Ori, but I don't think she's gonna listen to me."

Wrath walked back in the room and scowled at me. "Where the fuck is your bitch?"

"Oh my god, she's not my bitch. In fact, she's not a bitch at all. And maybe you could move into the twenty-first century and stop referring to women as bitches all together!"

"Would you prefer cunt?" Wrath seethed.

"You really are a fucking Neanderthal!" I squealed.

He knuckled his eyes, like he was warding off a headache, then took a deep breath. "Where's Sierra, Raquel?"

"She's at her ex's."

He fisted his hands at his sides. "The address," Wrath hissed.

"I'm not giving you the address." I glanced at Orion and moved closer to him.

"Give me the goddamn address," Wrath growled.

I shook my head. "She will absolutely lose her shit if I do."

"What the fuck's goin' on?" my brother demanded, walking into the room. "You better not be yellin' at my sister," he warned Wrath.

"Jesus fucking Christ!" Wrath jabbed a finger at Orion again. "Fuckin' deal with this."

He walked away with a curse.

"Sierra's missing," Orion explained.

"She's not missing," I countered.

"Why was no one watchin' her?" Tristan asked.

"She was at work," I said.

"Again," my brother stressed. "Why was no one watchin' her?"

"Scrappy was watching her," Orion said. "She slipped him."

"Of course she did," Tristan said with a groan.

"I'm gonna need that address, baby," Orion said to me.

"Don't give it to Wrath."

He sighed. "I'll have Aero get her."

"Can you get her?" I asked my brother.

"Knee-deep in somethin' else, sissy. If Aero can deal with it, I'd appreciate it."

I wrinkled my nose. "Fine."

He nodded, then headed back the way he came. I found Leith's info in my phone and sent it to Orion, then he sent it off to Aero before wrapping his arms around me and giving me a squeeze. "She's gonna be okay, Frazzle."

"Lordy, I hope so," I whispered.

"Tequila?"

I smiled up at him. "Yes. Definitely."

One hour later, I was snuggled up to Orion in the great room, sipping my third margarita when I heard my best friend wailing like a banshee, then Wrath appeared in the room with Sierra thrown over his shoulder like a sack of potatoes.

"Oh my god, what are you doing?" I snapped, standing.

"He's a fucking beast, Raquel!" Sierra hissed, trying to squirm out of his hold.

Wrath smacked her butt and I saw red. "Don't hit my friend!"

He ignored me and stomped up the stairs. I followed, Orion close on my heels.

"Let her go!" I demanded as Sierra pounded on his back.

Wrath spun to face me. "Your bi—*friend* is gonna be locked down."

"Where?"

"In my room," he said.

"Like hell I am!" Sierra spat out, pounding on his back

again. "Let me go!"

"Let her go!" I demanded, stepping toward him, but Orion pulled me back. I glared at him. "What are you doing?"

"Let Wrath deal with this."

"No way in hell!" I argued, turning to face them again and found they were no longer standing in the hallway. I pulled out of Orion's hold and rushed toward Wrath's room. The door was locked, so I pounded on it. "Open this door!"

"Raquel!" Sierra screamed, and I tried to force the door open. I kicked it, body slammed it, and got nothing but a bruised shoulder.

"Baby, quit!" Orion growled. "The door's solid wood, you're gonna hurt yourself."

"Get her out!" I ordered.

"Not gonna do that, Raquel. This is between Wrath and Sierra."

I faced him. "What the hell does that mean?"

"Baby—"

"Don't you dare 'baby' me," I snapped. "Get her out."

He sighed, banging on the door. "Wrath! Raquel would like to check on her friend."

"She can do that tomorrow," Wrath yelled in response.

"Raquel!" Sierra bellowed.

"Do something," I begged. "She's scared."

"She'll be okay."

"He's hurting her, though. You have to get her out."

"He's *not* hurting her, baby," Orion said. "He'd never hurt a woman, trust me. Just let them work it out."

I had never been so angry at another human being in my life. "I'm getting my brother."

"Not your brother's business, Razzle."

I pulled out my phone and texted him, despite Orion's decree.

154

"Are you seriously gonna tattle to your brother every time we have a disagreement?"

"This," I waved my hand between us, "is way beyond a disagreement," I snapped. "And since I trust him above anyone else, I think it's appropriate that I 'tattle' to him. If you're not gonna help my friend, then he will."

Heavy steps sounded on the stairs and my brother appeared like the badass savior he was. "What the fuck's going on?"

"Wrath has locked himself in with Sierra," I explained, calmly and without *overreacting*. "She doesn't want to be in there with him."

"She needs to be locked down, Raquel," Tristan said.

"She's not a criminal." I narrowed my eyes and crossed my arms. "Get her out."

Tristan banged on the door. "Wrath, brother, open the door."

"Fuck off, Doc."

"Proof of life, asshole, or I'm pulling rank."

"Fuck you," Wrath bellowed. "This isn't your house."

"Rank's rank, and you know it."

"Goddammit!"

The door flew open and I moved to walk in, but once again, Orion pulled me back. "Unhand me."

"Baby, your girl's good." He nodded into the room.

"Sierra?" my brother asked, leaning in. "You good?"

"Come on out," I directed.

Sierra slid off the bed and stalked toward me. "This man is an asshole."

"Sierra's going to sleep in my room."

"Ah, no, she's not," Orion countered.

"Yeah. She is."

"Raquel—"

"You can sleep with Wrath."

"Jesus," he hissed. "Don't overreact."

I scowled at him. "My best friend was accosted and locked in a room with a Neanderthal and you didn't do anything to help her, but I'm the one *overreacting*?"

"Bab—"

"Goodnight, *Adam.*"

Sierra and I walked up the stairs and closed ourselves into his room, locking both the door and the deadbolt.

"Why the hell would you go to Leith's?" I whisper-hissed, crossing my arms.

She shrugged. "Because he," she pointed toward the door, and I deduced she was referring to Wrath, "is not the boss of me. He has no right to tell me what to do."

"Okay, I get it, but Orion was the one who asked that you be here, not Wrath."

"Then why the hell is he the one dragging me everywhere?"

"That's a very good question." I sighed. "Did he hurt you?"

"No."

"I'll talk to Orion if he did."

"No. He was surprisingly gentle... for an asshole," she conceded.

"I'm sorry, honey."

"It is what it is," she said. "Well, I'm tired and I have an early shift tomorrow, so am I sleeping here?"

"Looks like it," I said. "But would you keep your clothes on? Just this once?"

Sierra always slept naked and I just couldn't deal with her accidentally spooning me in the middle of the night.

"Fine." She rolled her eyes. "Jesus, when did you get all prudish?"

"Not wanting you to dry hump me awake is not prudish."

"Me wearing panties to bed does not guarantee I won't dry hump you."

"And a T-shirt."

"A T-shirt won't save you either," she warned.

I groaned. "Oh my god."

We glanced at each other, then burst into uncontrollable giggles, and all was right with the world again.

Raquel

I AWOKE THE next morning to find Sierra gone. I had no idea where Orion was, but I honestly didn't really care at that moment. I was still angry and not quite ready to forgive him. I did, however, have a class at eleven, so I needed to get my ass out of bed.

I showered and dressed, then made my way downstairs, heading for the kitchen, hoping a pot of coffee was waiting for me.

"Hey, Raquel."

I turned to see Sundance walking in, a smile on his

face, a beanie on his now bald head.

"Hey. You're looking good." I poured a cup of coffee and then faced him again.

"Thanks. Chemo's a bitch, but today's a good day."

"What do the doctors say?"

"Won't know anything for a little while, but they're optimistic."

I let out a relieved sigh. "I'm really glad."

"Me too, sweetheart." He raised an eyebrow. "Heard there was a dustup last night. You okay?"

I rolled my eyes. "I'm not the one you have to worry about."

"I'll have a conversation with Sierra. Smooth things over."

"What?" I almost spit out my coffee. "I wasn't talking about Sierra."

"Oh?"

"You need to teach Wrath some manners."

Sundance laughed. "Not my job."

"Well, whose job is it?"

"You'll have to ask him."

"No thank you." I took a sip of coffee. "Where's Orion?"

Sundance frowned. "On his way to Denver, didn't he tell you?"

No, the little fucker did not *tell me.*

"I haven't checked my phone this morning," I lied. "He probably sent me a text."

"Probably."

My brother walked in and smiled. "Morning."

"Hi."

"You ready? I'm taking you to and from class today."

"Oh, okay." I nodded. "Let's go."

I grabbed a muffin from the pantry, poured my coffee into a travel cup, then followed Tristan out to my car.

"Am I allowed to drive, or do you need to do that, too?" I asked, my already bad mood spiraling into the toilet.

He raised an eyebrow. "You okay?"

"I'm peachy," I snapped.

"Can you drive with your hands bandaged?"

"Watch me," I retorted, hitting the unlock button on my key fob with my chin and sliding into the driver's seat.

Tristan climbed in beside me and I drove to my campus in silence, using my wrists most of the way, my anger swirling and stewing.

I parked, then climbed out, opening the back door and grabbing my bag as Tristan walked to the driver's side and held his hand out for the keys.

"I'll pick you up when you're ready. Just text me," he said.

"Whatever."

"That attitude's not directed at me, right?"

"I haven't decided yet."

He smiled. "Okay, well, I'm gonna leave you here. Maybe hit the attitude store before I pick you up."

"Oh, ha ha," I droned, wrinkling my nose.

He grinned. "I'll see you later. Go learn something."

"Go suck a bag—"

"Attitude store," he interrupted. "Buy the most expensive good one. Don't go generic."

I rolled my eyes and headed to class. When I had a break, I pulled my cell phone out of my bag and saw I had six texts from Orion and one missed call, but he hadn't left a voicemail.

So, I wasn't going to call or text him back.

He could learn to miss me for a minute.

* * *

When class was over, I texted my brother, then gathered

160

my books and shoved everything back in my bag. I knew it would take a few for him to get to me, so I didn't rush.

As I walked out to the parking lot, my heart raced as my stomach roiled. Orion stood in front of his bike, his head down, focused on his phone. My emotions warred with the excitement of seeing him and the fact I was still very pissed off.

I stalled, wondering if I could move fast enough to get back into the building without being seen. His head raised and he met my eyes, thwarting my plan to escape. He slid his phone into his pocket and gave me a chin lift.

I narrowed my eyes and continued to stand where I'd stopped, daring him to come to me. Neither of us moved, and I knew our game of chicken could go on forever. I pulled my phone out and called my brother. He answered on the first ring. "Is Orion not there?"

"Oh, he's here," I hissed. "But what I want to know is, why aren't you?"

He chuckled. "I see you didn't have time to go to the store."

"Tristan," I growled.

"Sissy, go talk to your man. You know I don't get in the middle of that shit."

"God, you're infuriating."

"I'm aware. Byeeeee."

He hung up and I stomped my foot in irritation, glancing at Orion who was smiling like an asshole.

I straightened my shoulders and made my way to him. "I'm calling an Uber."

He raised an eyebrow. "No, you're not. I'm taking you out."

"I'm sorry, I'm busy this evening."

"Oh, yeah?"

"Yep. I'm washing my hair."

He sighed. "Baby, don't be obstinate."

"Don't tell me how to live my life."

"Are you still pissed about last night?"

"A little."

"Okay, this level is more than a little, so you wanna fill me in on specifically what's crawled up your ass right now?"

"Oh, hell, no." I scowled, swiping my phone open again.

"Bab—"

"You did *not* just say that to me."

"As sexy as you are gettin' all southern on me, we need to talk, and I think Billy's would be a good place to do that."

My stomach rumbled, and he apparently heard it because he smiled in triumph.

"I can take a car to Billy's," I said.

"You're not takin' a fuckin' car to Billy's. You're gonna get your sweet ass on the back of my bike and press your pussy tight to me."

"I have yet to hear an apology from you, so until that happens, I'm going nowhere."

"What exactly am I apologizing for?" he asked. "Why don't you tell me so we can eat?"

"You're such an ass."

"I'm sorry for being an ass."

I let out a frustrated grunt. "Just take me back to the cabin. I need to study."

"*No*," he said slowly. "We're going to Billy's."

"Separate tables."

He grinned, leaning forward and stealing a kiss.

I swatted at him like I would a bug. "Get off me."

"We need to get to a place of peace before we get on my bike, baby, so give it to me."

"I don't feel like I should have to tell you what you should apologize for."

"I'm not a mind reader, Raquel, so help me out."

"You mean, besides the fact you were going to let a psycho keep my best friend prisoner?"

"Yeah, besides that."

"You left without telling me you were going to Denver after not sleeping with me last night."

"Do you need me to point out that your best friend was in bed with you, and believe me, baby, I've had a three-some, it's not all it's cracked up to be."

I wrinkled my nose. "You've had a threesome?"

"Focus, Razzle."

I frowned. "We're going to loop back to the threesome later."

He slid his hand to my neck. "I'm sorry I didn't let you know I was heading to Denver. It was last minute, and, honestly, if your brother wasn't here, I wouldn't have gone."

"What makes my brother so special?"

"He loves you almost as much as I do, which means, he will give his own life to protect you."

I refused to show him how much that sweet statement meant to me, so I licked my lips and tried for disinterest. "Did you get everything sorted you needed to?"

"Yes. For the moment." He stroked my cheek. "Missed you, though."

"Good."

He grinned. "Missed you more last night, if I'm being honest."

"Wrath didn't keep you warm?"

"Slept in the bunkroom, as you well know."

"It's a nice room."

"The beds are at least six inches too short for me."

"Oh, so you missed your bed, not me."

"Yes, sure, we can go with that," he retorted.

"I'm calling an Uber."

He chuckled, wrapping an arm tightly around me. "You're being ornery and any other day, I'd be all over that, but I'm starving."

My stomach grumbled again, and I tugged on his cut. "We can eat, I guess."

"Thank you." He kissed me again and this time, I reciprocated. "Jesus, I missed you," he whispered. "I'm sorry I didn't let you know I was heading to Denver."

"And?"

"I'm not apologizing for the Sierra thing, because she brought that on herself and Wrath never hurt or abused her. She was covered."

I sighed. He was right. Even Sierra confirmed that, so I suppose staying mad at him when Sierra was over it wasn't really fair.

"Fine," I said. "I'll let you have that one."

"Oh, thank you, your majesty."

I leaned back and raised an eyebrow. "Do you know the Warren Zevon song, 'Things to do in Denver when you're dead'?"

"Can't say that I do."

"Well, I highly suggest you listen to it, and take notes, because if you leave without telling me again, I'm going to murder you."

He dropped his head back and laughed, kissing me again, then handing me a helmet and stowing my bags before taking us to Billy's.

* * *

"Yes!" I hissed as Orion slammed into me from behind, slapping my ass once, then twice, bringing me to orgasm for the second time in less than twenty minutes.

I fell onto my stomach, but that didn't stop my man from burying himself deep, in fact, it gave him more leverage as he thrust into me harder. He bit down on my shoulder as his cock pulsed against my walls and I found myself orgasming again.

He kissed the place he'd just bit, then rolled us onto our sides. "That's three," he said.

I smiled, nodding as I licked my lips. "You can count. Well done."

He chuckled. "Top of my kindergarten class."

"You really missed me last night, huh? You're bringing your A-game."

"I always bring my A-game."

I laughed. "Right, sorry. Didn't mean to imply…"

"Better." Kissing my neck, he slid out of me, then headed to the bathroom.

I rolled to face the bathroom and sighed when he walked out, his dick still a little hard, and bit my lip.

"Like what you see?"

"So, so much," I breathed out.

He climbed back onto the bed and pulled me over his chest. "You've forgiven me, then?"

"Ask me in another three orgasms."

He kissed my temple. "Okay, baby, I'll work on that."

"Tell me about this threesome," I said.

"What do you want to know?"

"How many times have you…um…participated in one?"

"Twice."

"Seriously?"

"Yeah. The first time, I was pretty drunk and a little high, it was all about getting sucked off by two women and watching them go to town on each other. I was single, so were they, and it was hot as hell. The second time, though, I was practically sober and I made the mistake of letting my then girlfriend talk me into it."

"*She* suggested it?"

"Yeah." He cocked his head. "Baby, biker women can

be freaky."

"I know, but I've never known one willing to share."

"Yeah, I found that out mid-fuck," he admitted.

I gasped. "No way."

He grimaced. "Yeah. Needless to say, she and I broke up and I decided that it wasn't worth it. Nothing like that has happened for close to five years."

I raised an eyebrow. "Do you want it?"

"No." He stroked my back. "Honestly, it's all fun and games when you're single and high, but I've kind of always been a one woman man, so it was never my jam."

"Okay, good, because I will *never* suggest a threesome."

He chuckled. "I couldn't handle more than you anyway, so I appreciate that."

I rolled my eyes. "Did you talk to Wrath?"

"About what?"

I leaned up so I could meet his eyes. "Are you serious?"

"Razzle, I'm not gettin' in the middle of whatever he's got goin' with Sierra."

"He doesn't have anything going with Sierra, that's the point."

He settled a hand behind his head and raised an eyebrow. "You sure about that?"

"Um, yeah, she's my best friend. I'm pretty sure she'd tell me if she had a 'thing' going with Wrath."

He smiled. "Okay, Frazzle, maybe she doesn't."

"Then you need to talk to Wrath."

"Not gonna happen."

"Why not?" I sat up, the sheet falling away from me, leaving me fully exposed to him. I didn't miss the renewed look of desire as it blazed in his eyes, and I tried to pull the sheet around me again. I needed him to focus.

"Because it's none of my fuckin' business." He tugged

the sheet off me and grinned.

I tried to pull the sheet back, unsuccessfully. "If he's being an asshole to my best friend, shouldn't you make it your business?"

He cocked his head. "Define 'asshole.'"

"Ah, locking her in his room against her will is one definition."

"That was resolved."

I threw my bandaged hands in the air. "Because my *brother* pulled rank."

"Raquel, he didn't hurt her."

"Physically," I pointed out.

Sighing, he dragged his hands down his face. "I have never known Wrath to abuse a woman, mentally or otherwise."

"Oh, so throwing her over his shoulder and locking her —"

"Baby, if you did what Sierra did, you better fucking believe I'd throw you over *my* shoulder and lock you in my room. Would you consider that abuse?"

"Yes!" I cried.

"No, you wouldn't."

"How do you figure?"

"Because you know beyond a shadow of a doubt that I would never hurt you, and that my actions were born of a desperate need to protect you... even if it's from yourself."

"Wrath hates Sierra, so that doesn't apply."

"No, he doesn't."

"Well, she hates him."

He grinned...annoyingly. "No, she doesn't."

I let out a frustrated groan. "You are impossible."

He sat up, rolling one of my nipples between his finger and thumb. "So I've been told on numerous occasions."

Leaning forward, he sucked that same nipple into his mouth, then bit gently on it. I wanted to swat him away, but what he was doing to my nipples was rather delightful.

"Ori."

"Yeah, baby?" He moved to my other nipple and I dropped my head back.

"Sierra—"

"Is fine," he said, interrupting me again.

I grabbed his face and made him focus on something other than my breasts. "She needs to feel safe."

"Has she told you she doesn't?"

"Well, no, but—"

"She's in good hands, Frazzle. You can check in with her tomorrow, and if she says she doesn't feel safe, then I'll step in."

"Was that so hard?" I ground out.

"I'm gonna show you hard, baby," he said, flipping me onto my back and sliding into me.

"Ahhh," I cried out, and then he moved, burying himself deep as I wrapped my arms and legs around him, taking him fully.

"Jesus, I love your cunt."

"It loves you," I retorted, and he slammed into me harder and harder until I climaxed so hard my limbs contracted around him like a vice grip.

His orgasm came almost as quickly as mine, and he kissed me gently as we both came down from our high.

He stroked my cheek, kissing me once more. "Love you, beautiful."

I smiled. "Love you, too."

"You gonna shower with me?"

I nodded. "Yes, if you'll wash my hair."

He grinned. "I'm here at the pleasure of my queen."

"Damn straight."

Orion chuckled and after he secured plastic bags over my hands, he helped me into the shower. I had no idea that having my hair washed could be sensual, but Orion somehow managed to make it sexy as hell and gave me another orgasm in the shower before taking me back to bed.

I fell asleep against his naked body, fully sated.

Orion

THE NEXT MORNING, I dropped Raquel off at school, but not before she checked in with Sierra and made sure she was happy. Sierra assured her all was good, so Raquel let me escort her to class.

I had a feeling Sierra was more than good, but I chose to keep that to myself. Wrath had a certain reputation, and if Raquel suspected Sierra was wrapped up in any of that, my woman would probably lose her shit.

I rode out of the campus parking lot and headed south, away from the cabin and Monument. I needed to deal with something I'd been putting off and since Raquel was protected, as was Sierra, it was time I took care of some loose ends.

Pulling into the garage behind Durchester Park, I made sure my bike was out of sight and unlocked the back door of the building, stepping into the dark interior and giving my eyes a minute to adjust.

"Ori," Wrath called, and I followed the sound of his voice.

"You got 'im?" I asked.

"Yeah," he said. "Grimace is ready to back you up."

Grimace was big, close to six-foot-seven, and probably weighed three-hundred pounds. But it was all muscle. Mostly steroid-induced, which seemed to have shrunk his brain while it was beefing up his body. Although, the jury was out on whether or not Grimace was ever smart. If you looked in the dictionary under 'oaf,' his picture would be next to it, and although, he wasn't the sharpest tool in the shed, he was loyal, and I considered him a friend as well as a brother.

"Sundance said you cannot kill him."

"Sundance needs to mind his business," I hissed. "Why the fuck did you even tell him what I was doing?"

"You might be heir, brother, but he's still king."

"So, Grimace is here more to babysit me than provide backup."

"He's here to take your back, and if that means keeping you out of prison, more the better."

I sighed, then made my way down the hall and found Grimace leaning up against the wall.

"Hey, Ori."

"Hey." I smiled. "Looks like it's time to gut us a fish."

"Hell, yeah."

I pushed open the door and smiled. "Hey, Orca. How ya doin'?"

He was zip tied to a chair that was bolted into the con-

171

crete floor, his mouth duct taped shut, and it looked like he'd pissed himself.

"Orion figured we could start by seeing how well your gills work," Grimace said.

"Whales have blowholes, dumbass," I corrected.

"You just said it was time to gut a fish."

"It's a figure of speech. Orcas are technically whales, therefore mammals."

"Orcas are whales?"

"Jesus Christ, where did you go to school?" I asked.

"But Orca's not fat," he continued without answering my question.

"What are you talking about?"

"Well, if he's named after a whale, shouldn't he be a great big fat guy?"

"We're getting off topic here," I said, trying to keep my irritation at my biker brother under control. "Just fill up the fuckin' tub."

* * *

Raquel

I walked out of class as the sun was beginning to set. I hated Wednesdays. They were always long, and I'd get home practically unable to form sounds, let alone words.

I walked down to where I was supposed to meet Orion, but his bike wasn't there, and this gave me pause. In fact, I couldn't stop a shiver as I tried to find him in the sea of people.

"Raquel!"

I turned at the sound of my brother's voice and let out a sigh of relief. He was rushing toward me with a look of irritation on his face. "Am I late?"

"No," I said. "I got out a tiny bit early."

"Shit. Okay."

"What's wrong? Where's Orion?"

"We need to get you back to the cabin," he said without answering my question.

"Why?"

"Just trust me."

"Oh, my god, Tris, you're scaring me. What's going on?"

"I'm not goin' into details, sissy. Come on, let's just get you back."

He took my bag from me and led me to his rental car. I climbed in, but my stomach roiled, and I just wanted to get eyes on my man.

"Is Ori okay?" I whispered.

"Yeah, sissy, he's good."

I narrowed my eyes. "Have you seen him to confirm 'he's good'?"

"No."

"Oh, my god!" I squeaked. "What the hell is going on?"

"Jenae."

"What about my mom?"

"Well, she's here."

"What?" I asked on a gasp. "Here, where?"

"The cabin."

"No. Huh-uh. No way in hell."

"Way," my brother retorted.

"Why?"

"Because she went to the townhouse, where she was met by Scooby and Scrappy, and she demanded one of them take her to you."

I groaned. "My mother is not really at the cabin, surrounded by bikers...is she?"

He grinned. "'Fraid so, sissy."

"Jesus Christ. Did she remove her jewelry and hide her Birkin in the trunk?"

173

He glanced at me and nodded, his grin widening.

"Has she seen you yet?"

He couldn't stop his laughter as he shook his head and I smacked his arm.

"You did not really leave her there alone without at least reassuring her she was going to be okay, did you?"

He grimaced.

I couldn't blame him too much. My mother was a *snob*. With a capital S and had not always been kind to Tristan. He was the person who stood between her and our dad. He never did, but she always saw him as a threat.

Even twenty-eight years later, she was convinced my dad would leave her for a younger woman and that Tristan would help facilitate that. She was fifteen years my dad's junior, she had been a flight attendant, and since he was a pilot, she saw the bevy of offers he received on a daily basis, so I suppose it was a natural insecurity when she started to get older, but my mother was beautiful. Cindy Crawford beautiful.

"Oh, my god." I dropped my face into my hands. "You are such a *dick*."

"Guilty."

"Who's entertaining her?"

He leaned away from me. "Wrath."

"Holy shit, Tristan, drive!"

We were seconds from the gates of the compound, and I jumped out of the car almost before it had come to a complete stop, running into the cabin and almost slipping on the hardwood as I tried to stop myself from running into the wall.

"Mom?" I called as I walked in.

"Over here, honey."

I glanced around the room full of bikers and found her sitting in the corner with Sierra, a cup of tea in front of her and I bit my lip and smiled at my best friend who was the greatest human being on the planet.

I made my way over to them, and my mom stood, pulling me in for a hug. "What are you doing here?" I asked.

"My baby girl nearly dies in a fire and then doesn't tell me about it for days? You don't think I wouldn't rush my booty to her side to make sure she's okay?"

I blushed, dropping my head in contrition. "Sorry, Mama."

She sighed. "Now, what's this about the townhouse being fumigated?"

"Oh, uh, right."

"Termites," I said at the same time as Sierra said, "Roaches."

"Termites and roaches," I corrected. "It's sort of an infestation."

"Totally Biblical," Sierra interjected, and I gave her a look of warning. We did not need to go into any further detail to push my mother off the rails more than she was fixing to be.

"Oh, my word," Mom breathed out. "We paid prime money for that home. I'm going to need to call the insurance company."

"No," I rushed to say, maybe a bit aggressively. "Um, Orion's club is helping us out, so we don't need to get the insurance company involved."

"Why are you staying here?" she whispered. "I'd feel much better if you girls were in a hotel. I'll make a call and book you a room."

"No, Mama, it's okay."

All of a sudden, my mother's face twisted into both disgust and fear, and I turned to see Orion walking in, soaking wet and covered in blood.

"What the hell happened?" I cried, rushing to him, my mother quickly forgotten.

Orion frowned in my mother's direction and looked to

Wrath for answers.

"It's my mom," I whispered, annoyed he'd ignored my question.

"Fuck," he hissed.

"Why are you covered in blood?" I demanded, running my hands over his chest.

"It's not my blood, Frazzle," he whispered. "Give me a minute."

"No. I want answers, *Adam*," I growled.

He grabbed my wrists and bent down to get eye-to-eye with me. "I need to go get cleaned up so I can meet your mom without totally freaking her the fuck out. Wanna give me a few minutes to do that, or do you want to stand here and bust my balls with her continuing to watch?"

Tristan made his way to my mom and hugged her awkwardly. "Hey Jenae. Good to see you."

"What are you doing here?" she asked. "Where's Olivia?"

"She's home with the babies. I needed to do some continuing education, and there's a great course close by, so I figured I'd come and look in on Raquel." He nodded toward Orion. "Orion was helping me patch up one of the men who took a nasty spill on his bike."

I bit my lip to keep from squeaking. Lordy, I could kiss my brother right now.

"Mrs. Brooks, I'm just going to clean up so I can make a better first impression," Orion said, and I let him go, making my way back to my mom.

My mother appeared to be a bit flabbergasted as she focused back on Tristan. "You left your wife alone with twins?"

"No," he said, calmly. "She's surrounded by our family, including Dad, so she's covered."

"I bet she'd rather have you there."

"Oh, I know she would. But she also appreciates that I

have a career and that career requires I keep up with my license requirements." He raised an eyebrow. "I also wanted to make sure Raquel was okay, so I'm here."

Mom huffed, then pulled me aside. "I want you in a hotel."

"No, Mom, really," I said. "We won't be here for long."

She tugged me further into the corner. "Where are you sleeping?"

"There's a bunkroom here," Tristan said, and I gave him a look of total besotted appreciation for my big brother. I could never lie to my parents, even by omission. He had no problem doing it, even though, this wasn't technically a lie. There *was* a bunkroom here. He just didn't mention I wasn't sleeping in there.

"Does it have a lock on it?" Mom asked.

"Yes. Several," I said. "Big ones. But even if there weren't, there's nothing to worry about. No one here would ever lay a hand on me. I know it's hard to explain, but it's kind of like having a bunch of big brothers around."

"If you're into incest," Sierra retorted, albeit quietly.

I glared at her, hoping to god my mother didn't hear that.

"Mom, why don't we go to dinner? Somewhere nice," I suggested, just as Orion made his way to us, his clothing changed, but he couldn't hide his scraped-up knuckles, and I wished my mother wasn't here so I could find out exactly what the fuck happened.

"Probably best to stay here," Orion countered, and smiled his panty-dropping smile at my mother. "I'm so sorry I wasn't here to greet you properly. It's nice to finally meet you."

My mom gave him a weary smile. "You too."

"Please feel free to make yourself at home," Orion

177

said.

"I'd rather go somewhere…else. No offense."

"Some taken," Orion grumbled.

"Dinner sounds like a great plan," Mom continued.

"We actually have a club dinner planned today," Orion lied.

"Oh, well, that's perfect. I'll take Raquel and y'all can enjoy your club time."

"Raquel needs to be here," Orion insisted.

"I'm sure you can live without her for one dinner."

I faced Orion. "Surely, the Bistro's an option?"

He shook his head. "I'd rather we——"

"The Bistro sounds like a lovely place," my mother interrupted. "Shall we?"

"Actually, Mom, would you mind if I cleaned up a little?" I asked. "I have been in class all day and I'd really like to freshen up."

"Jenae, I'm dying to hear your story about the middle eastern sheik," Sierra said. "Maybe you can tell it while Raquel changes."

"Of course," Mom said, and I grinned at Sierra. I'm pretty sure I owed her a kidney.

"I won't be long," I promised, and headed up to Orion's room.

He followed, closing us in as I started pulling my shirt off.

"What the hell is going on?" I demanded in a whisper.

"Why are you whispering?" he asked with a smirk.

"Because my mother has the hearing of a bat." I grabbed one of his hands and ran my thumb gently over the knuckles. "What happened?"

"I don't want you leaving the compound, Razzle," Orion said, ignoring my question.

I dropped his hand and rummaged through the dresser drawer for a clean shirt. "Looks like we don't have much of a choice. My mom always gets what she wants, and what she wants is to take me to dinner."

He dragged his hands down his face. "Baby, it's church night. I can't come with you."

"I'm pretty sure you're not invited."

"Jesus," he hissed.

"Why are your hands all scraped up, Orion?"

"Babe—"

"*Adam,*" I ground out.

"You know, I'm starting to fuckin' hate my name," he ground out.

I frowned. "Why?"

He crossed his arms. "Because you only use it when you're pissed at me."

I sighed. "I'll try to use it when I'm super happy and in love with you, then."

"In other words, you're not super happy and in love with me now?"

"Who did you fight with?" I asked.

"Wasn't so much of a fight as a lesson."

"For whom?"

He studied me for a few tense seconds before he made the correct choice to tell me. "Orca."

I gasped. "Did you beat the shit out of Orca, or were you defending yourself?"

"That's all you're gettin', Raquel."

"And what kind of a mess is that going to cause?" I challenged.

"I made my bed and I'm gonna lay in it," he retorted.

"Did you change the sheets first?"

"Baby, no blowback." He dragged his hands through his hair. "He tried to fuckin' kill you. That shit cannot go unchallenged."

"Okay, fine. I get that, like Tristan, you're a biker, so you have a code. But why does this mean Mom and I can't drive the three miles to the Bistro and eat dinner together?"

"Because I can't be there."

"Then, Tris can come."

"He can't be there either."

"Right, church." I wrinkled my nose. "Okay, then who *can* come?"

"The only person available, who I trust, is Aero, but—"

"Great, we'll go with Aero," I said, pulling a T-shirt over my head. "He'll just have to make himself scarce."

"No." I faced him, and he shook his head. "It's not happening, Razzle."

I crossed my arms. "Do you really think Orca's club will come after me and Mom at the Bistro?"

"I'm not taking any chances."

I closed the distance between us and wrapped my arms around him, kissing the base of this throat. "Smoky, we'll be fine. The restaurant's less than five miles away."

"That's not really the point."

"*Please* let me have a dinner away from the compound with my mom." I ran my tongue over his pulse. "I need out."

He sighed, sliding his hands into my hair. "Let me see if I can send Grimace for backup."

I grinned up at him. "Thanks, honey."

"Don't make me regret this."

"I promise I will not let either of us get hurt."

He kissed me again and then led me back downstairs, where he promptly pressed me against the wall and gave me a brief make-out session away from prying eyes.

"Ew, isn't he like your 'big brother'?"

Well, so much for that. I broke our kiss and raised an eyebrow at my best friend.

She glanced around. "Last I checked, we were in Colorado, not Kentucky. Did you beam me up?"

I rolled my eyes. "Aren't you supposed to be babysitting my mom?"

"She invited me to go with you, so I'm going to put on a little makeup."

I smiled. "Awesome."

"I'll be quick."

Orion and I walked into the great room where Tristan was now entertaining my mom. Well, until Wrath totally lost his shit.

"No fucking way," he bellowed. "Goddammit! This is bullshit!"

He stalked through the room and stormed up the stairs.

I glanced up at Orion and he leaned down and whispered, "Looks like Wrath found out Sierra was going with you."

I raised my eyebrows in shock. "*That* was for Sierra?"

He nodded. "Like I said, baby, he's all about keeping her safe."

A few minutes later, Sierra came bounding down the stairs, looking like she was primed for murder. "You need to curb your dog," she snapped at Orion, jabbing a finger at him.

"Not really in my job description, sweetheart."

"Is this what it's like here every night?" my mother demanded, her nose in the air and her lips pursed in disapproval.

"No," I said emphatically.

"I think we should go," Mom continued. "Now."

I sighed, leaning on my tiptoes to kiss Orion quickly, then following my mother and Sierra out to Mom's rental car. The roar of pipes sounded behind us and I glanced back, seeing Wrath and Aero following, instead of Grimace and Aero.

"Is he serious?" Sierra hissed.

"Why are those motorcycles following us?" Mom asked.

"Orion wants to ensure we make it to the restaurant safely."

"Why wouldn't we be safe?"

"No reason, Mama," I assured. "It's their way of looking out for us."

"Or stalking us," Sierra muttered.

"What was that honey?" Mom asked.

"Oh, nothing, Jenae. It's all good," Sierra said.

We drove to the restaurant without incident, and I noticed that Wrath and Aero stuck around. In fact, they walked into the restaurant and got a table.

Next to us.

"Are they really going to eat with us?" Mom asked.

"They're not technically eating with us, Mom. It's fine, just ignore them."

I made sure she took the chair with her back to them, while I sat across from her with Sierra in between. It wasn't lost on me that Wrath changed his seat so he could be closer to Sierra, and I don't think it was lost on her either, with the glare she was aiming his way.

"What's good here?" Mom asked, perusing her menu.

"Everything," I said, kicking Sierra under the table who was still glaring daggers at Wrath.

Wrath grinned wide and Sierra reluctantly focused back on her menu.

Raquel

W E SURVIVED DINNER, sort of. Sierra went to the restroom, a *lot*. So much so, Mom began to worry she had dysentery. What made it even more awkward was that Wrath followed her. Every time.

"I'd really like you to come back with me," Mom said as we headed back to her car.

Wrath had insisted Sierra go with him, so Mom and I were alone.

"I can't, Mama. I have to study."

"I came all this way to spend some time with my girl, surely you can take some time off," she said as we parked in front of the cabin.

I stuffed down my frustration as I faced her before getting out of the car. "I love you. To the moon and back, you know that. But I'm struggling a little with the curriculum this semester and I need to pass these two classes, or I might not graduate."

She sighed. "Daddy mentioned that."

I gave her arm a squeeze. "Are you okay? If you know I'm knee-deep in this crap, what possessed you to come all the way here when I can't spend time with you?"

She dropped her head.

"Mama, what's wrong?" I whispered.

She took a deep breath and met my eyes. "I'm being extorted."

"What?" I squeaked as we made our way up to the cabin porch.

Her face flushed and she looked at the ground again. "A sex tape. Taken before your father and I got involved."

Okay, I was gonna need a few more hours and a lot of tequila to process that.

Moving on.

"You need Tristan's help, don't you? So you used me being here as an excuse to talk to him." I sighed. "Mom, you could have just called him. He'll help you."

She shook her head. "I can't call him. My phone's been cloned or hacked or something. He's listening to everything."

"He. So you know who he is?"

She nodded.

"Who?"

She blinked back tears. "Gary."

I gasped. "*Uncle* Gary?"

She blushed even redder and my stomach roiled. Gary was my dad's older brother and he'd always been a creep, which was why I had only met him a handful of times.

"Oh, my god, you slept with Uncle Gary?"

"He forced me."

"He raped you?"

"Well, no, technically it wasn't rape. I agreed." She met my eyes again. "Baby, I do not want to go into detail with you on this. It was a bad time, and I will not be able to live with myself if your opinion of me changes."

I pulled her in for a hug. "Mama, nothing you do will change my love for you. Well, unless you cheat on Daddy, of course." I leaned back and met her eyes. "Oh, my god, did you cheat on Daddy?"

"I would *never*," she hissed out. "He and you kids are my world."

The front door opened and Tristan stood in the doorway. "Hey. You okay?"

"Mom needs your help," I blurted.

"Raquel," Mom said on a groan.

"Uncle Gary's extorting her," I continued.

"Jesus," Tristan hissed. "He always was an asshole."

Mom's shoulders dropped in relief. "He was? I mean, he's always been an asshole to me, but I thought you were close."

"Who the fuck led you to believe I was close to that degenerate piece of shit?" Tristan spit out.

Mom bit her lip and shook her head. "He did."

"Right, so, now that you have considered the source, wanna fill me in on why you didn't come to me sooner?"

"Can we maybe not do this on the porch?" I asked. "Where's Orion?"

"He's in the kitchen."

"I'll leave you two to talk," I said and went looking for my man.

He was in the kitchen grabbing a beer from the fridge and I took a minute to admire his ass before saying, "For someone so totally obsessed with my safety, I'd like to know why you weren't waiting on the front porch for me."

He grinned, closing the fridge and wrapping an arm around my waist, kissing me quickly. "Wrath got here ten minutes before you, and Mozart let me know the second you came through the gate, but your brother wanted to be the one to greet you first, so I let him."

I wrinkled my nose. "I'd like the record to reflect, I don't like that."

He chuckled, giving me a squeeze. "Noted."

"How pissed was Sierra?" I asked.

"She was half-naked by the time I saw them, so I think she was fine."

"Oh my god, seriously?"

"Yeah, baby. I think you need to wrap your mind around the fact your girl is fuckin' Wrath. And enjoyin' it."

I shook my head and changed the subject. "How was church?"

He smiled. "How was dinner?" he asked, ignoring my question.

"Weird." I leaned heavily against him. "I wish I'd stayed here."

"Why? What's goin' on?"

I shook my head. "Not here."

He lifted my chin and frowned. "That bad?"

I nodded, and he took my hand and pulled me into one of the bunk rooms, closing the door behind us and crossing his arms. "What's wrong?"

I filled him in on what I knew about my mom's situation and he scowled. "Your brother's on this?"

I nodded.

"You want me to step in?"

Seriously, I loved this man beyond reason. "No, baby, it's all good."

He hooked his hand around my neck and tugged me forward, wrapping his arms around me and kissing the top of my head. "How are your hands?"

"Better," I said, hugging him tight.

He gripped my hair and guided my head back so I could meet his eyes. "You lyin' to me?"

I rolled my eyes. "No. They really do feel better. Tristan thinks the bandages can come off in a few days."

"I know. He told me."

"Then what do you need me for? You apparently have all the answers before you ask the questions," I retorted.

He chuckled, leaning down to kiss me. "I got your brother's answer, but I still didn't have yours. I'm relieved to hear they're the same."

I sighed, kissing him again. "I can't believe my mom made a sex tape."

"Sounds like she didn't know it was happening."

"True. But I couldn't imagine having something so personal out there." I shuddered. "And she fucked my gross uncle. That's beyond creepy."

"We're gonna deal with him, baby. Your mom's covered. Don't doubt it."

I nodded and looked up at him. "Don't kill him."

"Not making any promises."

I sighed. "I'm okay with you roughing him up, but don't kill him. That would be too easy."

"I'll keep your opinion in mind," he said. "For now, though, I want to kill your pussy. You up for that?"

"Yes," I hissed. "Mom's gonna be busy for a bit, so we have time."

He leaned back and locked the door. "Strip."

I bit my lip and did as he demanded.

* * *

Orion

Some time around two a.m., I left Raquel in my bed and

headed downstairs to meet with Doc and Rabbit. I had a feeling I'd get pulled into the shit with Raquel's mom, particularly because Gary apparently lived in Denver, so it made sense for us to deal with him.

I walked into my office to find Rabbit hunkered down in a chair, his feet on my desk, and a laptop on his lap, with Doc leaning down behind him, reading something on the screen.

"Whatya got?" I asked.

"I hacked into his personal cloud," Rabbit said. "But I don't wanna look at it. Jenae's hot as fuck, but I got too much respect for Doc's dad to watch his wife doin' the nasty."

"And I seriously don't want to watch it," Doc admitted. "No interest in seein' my step-mother fuckin' my ugly fatass uncle."

"Can't you just delete it?" I asked.

Rabbit shook his head. "He's got a trigger built in that will notify him if someone tries, which makes me believe this isn't the only copy."

"Jesus," I said. "I'm not watchin' it."

"Well, someone needs to watch it," Rabbit said. "We need to know what we're dealin' with."

I really didn't want to see my woman's mother in a compromising position. I sighed and pulled out my phone, firing off a text. It took less than five minutes for Wrath to come strolling into the room, shit eating grin on his face. "You got a porno for me to look at?"

"Sex tape. Taken against the woman's will, so let's keep that in perspective," Doc warned.

I had to give my road captain credit, he faked a serious and concerned expression as Rabbit handed him the laptop and pressed the play button.

"Holy fuck!" he snapped. "Is that Raquel's mom?"

"Focus, brother," I instructed. "We need to know what

we're dealin' with here."

"Well, her tits are obviously a solid C-cup, she's got a tiny waist and an ass that bounces when she moves. Jesus, she's hot as fuck."

"Okay, that's enough," Doc said, and pushed the laptop closed.

"We need him to watch the whole thing," Rabbit pressed.

"Fuck me," Doc said. "I don't want Jenae exploited."

"Sorry, man, I get it," Wrath said. "I'll keep my thoughts to myself."

Doc removed his hand and Wrath opened the computer again, firing up the video. He kept the sound up and I cringed hearing Jenae sobbing quietly in the background while the asshole grunted as he fucked her.

Jesus, I couldn't wait to get my hands around the asshole's neck.

"This is obvious proof she wasn't enjoying any of that," I said, unable to continue to listen.

"Yeah," Doc agreed. "But she's scared to death to go to the cops because Gary's threatened to kill Raquel."

My blood boiled. "He's threatened Raquel?"

Doc sighed. "Yeah."

"Way to bury the fuckin' lead, Doc," I bellowed. "Jesus Christ!"

"She's covered."

"Yeah, I know she's fuckin' covered. *I've* got her covered," I growled. "If this guy so much as sneezes in her direction, I'll rip his dick off."

"I'll help you hide his balls," Doc said. "But we need a solid plan so we can figure out how to solve this with no blowback."

"I'll tell you what we're gonna do. *I'm* gonna drive up to Denver and deal with it."

"Has Jenae told your dad what's goin' on?" Rabbit

asked.

Doc shook his head. "Gary's threat extends to my dad as well."

"Okay," I said. "Road trip to Denver. Tomorrow."

"Yeah," Doc and Rabbit said in stereo.

* * *

I dropped Raquel at class the next morning, glad it was a full day of school for her, then I met up with Doc and Rabbit, riding borrowed bikes. We headed up to Denver, making it in less than forty-five minutes, and following the GPS to Gary's condo in one of the downtown high rises.

We arrived to find the lobby empty. We'd expected a doorman, but no one was around, so we took the opportunity to grab an elevator and make our way to Gary's floor. I'd kind of hoped Doc would be able to help guide us, but he hadn't seen his uncle in fifteen years, and had never been here, so we were all flying blind.

Stepping into the tenth floor hallway, we approached number 1012, finding the door slightly ajar. I turned to face Doc and he nodded, indicating to go slow. We all pulled our guns out of our holsters and inched through the door, finding the condo in disarray, and a blood trail leading from the kitchen. We followed the trail and pushed into the bathroom. Gary's lifeless and bloody body was sprawled out on the floor, a man standing over him with a hunting knife.

"Shit," Doc hissed. "Dad?"

* * *

Raquel

I walked out of class to find Aero waiting for me in Sundance's truck. I sighed. "Where's Orion?"

"He had shit to do."

"And my brother?"

Aero reached his hand out. "Can I take your bag?"

"They're together, I take it?" I mused, handing my backpack over.

"In the truck, Raquel."

I rolled my eyes and climbed in, securing my seatbelt and pulling my phone out, sending Orion a quick text. Not that I expected a response.

My brother had given the okay to remove my left bandage, as that hand was healing the fastest, so I was able to do a few things, although, not easily since it wasn't my dominant hand. At least I could text now. It made things much easier.

"Can you take me to the Hilton, please?"

"No," Aero said.

"Why not?"

"Got orders to get you back to the cabin."

"Orion's not even there," I argued. "I'd like to spend the evening with my mother."

"No can-do, sweetheart."

My phone buzzed just as I was about to go crazy banshee on him. It was my mom, so I answered. "Hi, Mom. Were your ears burning?"

"Gary's dead."

"What?" I whispered.

"It was on the news."

"This soon?"

"The editor-in-chief of the Denver Chronicle just happens to live in your uncle's building."

"Convenient," I murmured.

"I need you here, honey."

Aero shook his head.

"Can you come to the cabin instead?"

"I don't really fit in with those people."

"Mama, don't be difficult. I'll come and pick you up."

Aero scowled and I muted my phone, letting my mom continue to argue one-sided.

"I'm not letting her Uber," I said.

"Jesus, Raquel, Orion's gonna have my head if I deviate from the plan."

"And I'll have yours if you don't. Pick which one of us you're more afraid of, but understand that if anything happens to my mother because you chose to leave her stranded, I will cut your dick off and choke you with it."

"Raquel, are you still there?" Mom asked.

Aero raised an eyebrow as I unmuted my phone, and smiled when he flipped a U-turn. "I'm here, Mom. I'm coming to get you. Please pack an overnight bag."

"Raquel—"

I hung up on her. I had never done that before, but I just couldn't listen to her argue with me anymore. I needed her in the compound and safe.

Aero drove up to the hotel and parked, then walked me up to Mom's room where she was none too pleased to be forced to leave the 'comfort of her hotel for a den of iniquity.'

"You'll love the den," Aero assured. "I'll keep you plied with tequila."

I bit back a laugh. I had never seen my mother drunk, but I suddenly wanted to.

She huffed, dropping her bag at Aero's feet and striding out the door. He grabbed her bag and then we made our way back to his truck.

Once we were back in the safety of the compound, I let myself relax slightly, although, I was pissed beyond reason.

I knew exactly who had killed Gary and I was *not* happy about it.

Raquel

THE BED DIPPING awakened me and I frowned. "Who's there?"

"It's me," Orion said.

"I locked that door."

"Yeah, I figured that out."

"But you chose to break in anyway?"

"It's my room," he pointed out.

"Well, I would like you to sleep somewhere else."

"Not happenin'."

I threw the covers off and sat up. "Then I will."

"What crawled up your ass, Frazzle?"

"Are you kidding me?"

"No, baby. What I am is wiped out and just want to crawl into bed with my woman."

"I'm not sleeping with a murderer."

"Jesus," he hissed.

"I specifically told you I didn't want you to kill him! Now I'm going to have to decide if I'm going to have time to visit you in the pen."

"It's good to know you'll at least try," he retorted.

"Oh my god, Adam, this is not funny."

He pushed me onto my back and hovered over me. "I didn't kill your uncle, baby."

"Right."

"It wasn't me," he said.

"Then who did?"

"Not gonna go there, Razzle. You can talk to your brother in the morning."

"My *brother* killed him?" I squeaked, pushing at Orion's shoulders.

He shook his head. "Tomorrow, Raquel."

"Let me up."

"Babe—"

"Move." I shoved at his shoulders again. "Please."

He rolled off, albeit reluctantly, and I dragged on a pair of sweats.

"Where is he?"

Orion dragged his hands down his face. "Last I saw him, he was in the bunkroom by the kitchen."

I flew out the door and downstairs, banging on the door of the bunkroom and pushing in before I was given permission to enter.

And then I froze.

My brother was stitching up a wound on my father's arm and it took me a minute to register that my father was here.

"Daddy?"

"Jesus," my brother hissed. "I thought you were keeping her out of this, Orion."

"Yeah, I tried," Orion said from behind me.

"Keeping me out of what?" I snapped. "I already figured out you killed Gary."

"It wasn't your brother, chickpea," Dad countered.

"Oh my god," I ground out, glaring up at Orion. "You lied to me?"

He frowned. "I have never lied to you."

"It was me, chickpea," Dad said.

"What was you?"

"I killed Gary."

Chalk it up to exhaustion and the fact it was dark o'clock in the morning, but I couldn't quite wrap my mind around what my father had just said.

"I'm sorry? Wait, where's Mom?"

"Asleep, I hope," Dad said.

Orion, wrapped an arm around me from behind. "Baby, come to bed. You can process all this tomorrow."

"You killed Uncle Gary?" I rasped. "Why?"

"Razzle, I'll fill you in in the morning," Orion pressed.

"No," I growled. "What the hell is going on?"

"I really need you to take a beat, chickpea," Dad said.

Orion turned me to face him and stroked my cheek. "Come to bed."

I blinked back tears, dropping my head to his chest. "I want to know what's going on."

"And I promise I'll tell you," he said. "But right now, you need to rest."

I sighed, leaning heavily against him.

"Come on, baby, let's go upstairs."

I let him lead me upstairs, closing us into his room and I lost my hold on my emotions, bursting into tears and fisting my hands in Orion's T-shirt. "Did my dad really murder someone?"

"Legally, it was self-defense."

"But it wasn't really, was it?"

"Baby, your uncle raped his woman. Do you really think he'd let that stand?"

"My dad's a pilot, Smoky. Not a biker. I figured he'd find a way to deal with him that was less violent."

"Your brothers are a product of your father's raising. The apples don't fall far from the tree."

I nodded into his T-shirt. "I know this sounds crazy, but I'm kind of glad he was the one who dealt with it."

"It doesn't sound crazy."

I met his eyes. "He totally protected my mom."

"Did you expect anything less?"

"Yes, obviously, but I'm glad I was wrong. Although, I'm not sure how I feel about him killing someone."

"Bullshit."

"What?"

"You know exactly how you feel." He fisted his hand in my hair and guided my head back so we were eye-to-eye. "You're not blind to biker life, Razzle. You know the code, so don't pretend you don't."

"Don't tell me how to feel," I snapped.

"Settle down, garbanzo bean," Orion retorted.

"Suck a bag of dicks, *Adam*."

He smiled, kissing me quickly. "Jesus, you're fuckin' gorgeous when you're pissed off."

"Oh, this is mildly annoyed. I haven't hit pissed off yet. But keep goin', buddy, you're driving me there imminently."

"I'm not telling you how to feel, baby, I'm simply pointing out that you're not being entirely truthful with your disdain and shock."

"How do you figure?"

"Your dad might be a pilot, but you know he's alpha to the core, so he's gonna treat each situation accordingly. You know Doc's gonna fuckin' take care of his business and your younger brothers are already doin' the same. Your dad raised those men, so I don't really think you're all that surprised that your dad defended your mother's honor at the end of a knife."

"He used a knife?"

"Focus, Frazzle."

I wrinkled my nose, but kept quiet.

"Your dad protected his family. No less than what me or Doc would have done."

I sighed, dropping my head to his chest again. "I know."

"So my only question is, are you going to lean in or freak out?"

"I can't do both?"

He chuckled. "Nope. You gotta pick one, baby. If you lean in, though, I'll make sure it's worth your while."

I bit my lip and smiled up at him. "I'm fixin' to lean in, Smoky. Better get your dick ready to make it worth my while."

He laughed, lifting me and throwing me on the bed, pulling my sweats and panties off and burying his face between my legs.

I leaned in. And sideways, and he definitely made it worth my while.

Raquel

Two years later...

I SET THE pregnancy test stick on the counter and washed my hands. Orion was at the warehouse checking on the progress of our new strain he affectionately called 'Razzle Dazzle' in honor of my research. We had already extracted a liquid that was working beautifully on adults with challenges, and he had plans to make edibles and wax in the near future.

We'd been married a little over a year ago, and our life was close to perfect in my opinion. We'd had the wedding of my dreams with Orion's club, my brother's club, family and friends all in attendance. Sierra, Violet, and Olivia were my bridesmaids and Orion had his brother, dad, and Tristan as his groomsmen. My younger brothers acted as ushers, although, they were somewhat useless at keeping any kind of order. Not that I judged them too harshly. How do you keep bikers from stomping all over the white carpet runner when you're only nineteen and twenty-one years old? It's not easy.

I'd made the mistake of popping an edible before we said our vows, so I found myself giggling a lot through the ceremony. When the preacher had said, "You may kiss your bride," I had a different idea, running my tongue up Orion's cheek and announcing, "I licked him, he's mine."

Orion's family (and the few friends who knew them well) burst into belly laughs, then Orion pulled me in for an epic wedding kiss that was full of love, promise, and tongue.

Sundance had insisted we take one of the cabins on the compound property, rather than looking for a home outside the walls. From the little Orion shared, I knew the club was fixing for a war they didn't want, but ultimately had been forced to participate in with the Predators, so it made sense they wanted us close and within the safety of the compound. Orca's mutilated corpse had been found deep in the woods and the cops determined it to be a hiking accident, his body picked at by predators. I knew better, but kept that knowledge to myself.

Since we figured we'd be here a while, we'd picked the biggest cabin, mostly because it had been gutted a few years ago, so it was a blank canvas. It took six months to make it the home we both wanted and needed, and I loved every inch of it. We had three bedrooms plus a den, three and half bathrooms, along with a huge kitchen and great room. Orion and his dad had attached a three-car garage to the side of the cabin, giving us access via the laundry room which they'd expanded and made more of a mud room.

My mom wasn't too thrilled with me living in Colorado permanently, but Dad promised to fly her here anytime she wanted, so she stopped harping on me. Sort of.

"Babe?" Orion called and I grabbed the stick and made my way to the kitchen.

"Hey, Smoky," I said.

He kissed me gently. "What are you hiding behind your back?"

"Okay, you know how I keep crying all the time?"

"Nope," he deadpanned. "I have never known you to be anything but even-keeled."

I grinned. "And my nipples are extra sensitive?"

"Not to mention your tits have doubled in size."

"They have not."

"Yeah, baby, they have. It's like you're preg—wait, are you pregnant?"

"Let's find out together." I pulled the stick out and held it up.

Orion leaned closer. "What do the two lines mean?"

"It means that in about eight months, you're gonna be a daddy."

"Fuck, seriously?"

"Yep."

He threw his arms around me, picking me up and spinning me in a circle. "I fucking love you, baby."

I laughed. "I fucking love you too, Smoky."

Setting me on my feet, he kissed me, laying his hand on my belly. "Our very own little howler."

"I can't wait."

"Me neither," he said, kneeling in front of me and kissing my belly. "Listen here, little pup, you need to go easy on your mama. No making her sick or growing so fast her back goes out."

I giggled, sliding my hands into Orion's hair.

"And no fucking coming early," he continued. "You will cook the adequate amount of time and be healthy."

I groaned. "Baby, I'm not baking a cake."

He looked up at me. "No, it's way more important than that. You're baking a human."

I grinned and cupped his chin. "I suppose you're right."

He rose to his feet and kissed me gently. "So fuckin' proud of you, sweetheart."

I grinned. "Back atya."

"Are we going out or am I cooking?"

"Out," I said. "Definitely out."

"Bistro?"

"Yes, please," I said.

"I'll clean up and we'll go."

He kissed me again and went to clean up.

* * *

Eight and a half months later...

"Your little baby cretin is late," I complained, inching my way down the stairs of our home. My ankles were the size of my thighs, and I could barely move without waddling in discomfort.

Orion smiled gently from the bottom of the stairs and held his hand out. "I know, baby. You'll be induced tomorrow and all of this will be over."

"I don't want to wait—" Sudden wetness flooded against my thighs and I froze. "Shit. I peed again."

"I don't think that's pee, Razzle," Orion countered.

I glanced down and could barely see over my belly a huge puddle at my feet. "Oh, my god, I think my water broke."

He grinned. "Looks like it. Come on, Razzle, we'll get you to the hospital."

"Call Mom."

My mother had run up to the main cabin to grab a set of keys for the cabin next to us. My whole family would be descending upon us the day after tomorrow and Mom wanted to stock it with food.

Doc and Olivia were already here with the twins, but they'd opted to stay in the main cabin, so there'd be more room for Mom, Dad, and my brothers

"I will, baby," Orion promised, his cell phone already out of his pocket.

"And Tristan."

"On it," he promised, helping me to my car and helping me inside before securing my seatbelt.

"I need my bag."

"I'll get it."

"And my purse."

He grinned, kissing me gently. "I'll get everything, Frazzle. Don't worry."

He left me briefly to grab everything I needed and then we drove to the hospital where I was quickly settled into a birthing room.

Tristan and Olivia arrived a few minutes later with my mom and I settled in for what I expected would be a long labor.

I was wrong.

Luca Thorne Graves arrived two hours later, nine pounds six ounces, and twenty-three inches long, perfectly pink and healthy, with a quick howl, then a quiet cool that I was sure he'd inherited from his daddy.

"He's perfect," I whispered, smiling down at my beautiful little boy with the ice blue eyes. Luca stared up at me and then his lips began to purse, so I settled him to my breast and he took the sustenance my body offered.

"You're perfect," Orion said, leaning down to kiss me. "Thank you."

I reached up and stroked his beard. "You're welcome."

As our family filtered in and out of my room, greeting its newest member, I held tight to my husband and baby, sending up a silent prayer of thanks for the perfection that I'd been given.

I was beyond blessed.

Piper Davenport writes from a place of passion and intrigue, combining elements of romance and suspense with strong modern-day heroes and heroines.

She currently resides in pseudonymia under the dutiful watch of the Writers Protection Agency.

Like Piper's FB page and get to know her!
(www.facebook.com/piperdavenport)

Twitter: @piper_davenport

CPSIA information can be obtained
at www.ICGtesting.com
Printed in the USA
LVHW040910301119
638508LV00002B/195